Going Down

Going Down

John St. Robert

Writers Club Press
San Jose New York Lincoln Shanghai

Going Down

Writers Club Press
an imprint of iUniverse, Inc.

For information address:
iUniverse, Inc.
5220 S. 16th St., Suite 200
Lincoln, NE 68512
www.iuniverse.com

ISBN: 0-595-20981-5

Printed in the United States of America

Many thanks to my wife and family, and to my undisclosed sources in inspiring me to write this story.

CHAPTER 1

John McNair awoke suddenly to another day of sunshine, yawned and punched his pillow to soften it up. He nearly forgot what day it was until his attempt at dozing off again was interrupted by some alarming thoughts and a very noisy alarm clock. He opened an eye to peek at the clock, but knew in his gut that this was exactly when his plan of intrigue and maybe death was to begin.

The impact would be quite far reaching, he realized, involving a variety of very important people. Included were many from his former home in Montreal, his associates in Minnesota, and his compatriots at his current place of business in the mostly sunny, but occasionally cloudy and cool, Bahamas. He knew the islands well, having resided in Nassau for the past four years while mingling with the most affluent money makers and exchangers.

McNair, however, didn't have much time to think in bed or bask in the balmy Bahama sunlight already beginning to sneak through his curtains that morning. His plan called for quick action. First, he must contact a tiny airport on the outskirts of nearby Bimini to see if his delivery schedules were still on time. And second, he must be sure everything was arranged up north.

As an officer of the International Canadian Bank branch in Nassau, it was important that he make these calls very discreetly. He used only the name Pelot-sounding somewhat like pillow. Whether

1

this was a first name or last was unknown by those contacted—but everyone he called always knew immediately and precisely what he wanted and how to respond.

This time his call north would go all the way to a bedroom in St. Paul, Minnesota where a very important judge—Francis J. Sims—was waiting. He was regarded as a key player in keeping Bahamian bankers happy as well as many others on the islands who McNair jokingly referred to as "addict freaks," but seriously regarded as "very, very good customers."

When the phone rang for Judge Sims, another dreary fall day in St. Paul was appearing over the horizon. The call came at 6:45 a.m.—an hour earlier than Bahama time. As usual, the judge was reclining on his favorite chair in his bedroom with an unlit cigar in his mouth. Bedecked in very colorful polka dot pajamas, he continued to peer out a panoramic window overlooking his private lake through high-powered binoculars until the ringing stopped. As usual, only the words Pelot were left on his Caller-ID—without any numbers to call back. But the judge knew there would be no message and that this was just a "signal of deliverance."

Instead of reacting hastily, the judge pondered awhile that October morning, seemingly irritated over being interrupted in viewing the peaceful and interesting scenery outdoors. Usually around the end of autumn Minnesota wildlife is as active as the falling leaves. In general, however, the weather there can be described as mostly gray. Unlike the Bahamas, where temperatures hover around 72 to 80 in fall, Minnesota weather is often around the low 50s and 60s. And unlike Minnesota's near freezing lakes, Bahama water temperature usually floats around the 80s.

Both sky and water around the Twin Cities were partially covered with birds when Pelot's call came, with many flying south over Sims' bedroom community. He knew dismal weather could hang around for days. Many in the state were eager for it to brighten up so they could lighten up. But for Sims, it was like a premonition that things could remain gloomy for the day. His plans had no ray of hope for anything brighter or better. In fact, Sims' usual self-assured attitude somewhat flickered out with the phone call. It was as if he knew this could be his last day on earth.

Even before hearing from McNair, however, this distinguished justice of the Minnesota Supreme Court already seemed somewhat depressed. It is rather natural to feel this way at times for Minnesotans with the approach of another predicted wicked winter. For many, it's often difficult to remember that when, and if, the sun does come out, the Twin Cities area can sometimes resemble a picturesque post card. Colorful foliage around its attractive lakes, mirrored on clear water under blue sky and soft puffy clouds with birds, can reflect a beautiful mural of departing autumn days.

But realistically, the low-flying fowl on fall mornings in the "Gopher State" are often noisy Canadian geese honking goodbyes as they head to warmer climes. Although a few of the sleepy residents near Sims' exclusive area that morning were probably envious being unable to also fly away from their hum-drum work-a-day world soon to begin, many of his so-called "snow bird" neighbors were very financially able to take flight and could also be called "early birds" able to catch the sun wherever it moved.

As an environmentalist, the judge was up extra early not only to hear the phone but to see and hear the geese that seemed especially loud as approaching dark clouds began to threaten his community once again. Although there seemed no way to escape, a grin appeared on Sims' face when he thought of all the die-hard golfers he knew who were eager to swing their clubs one more time before the closing of their popular high-priced country club courses. He knew they may indeed be cursing, thinking about the bird droppings already piling up around the ponds, fairways and manicured greens of their well-kept private golf links.

The judge, especially known for his harsh treatment of criminals throughout the state, observed nature as very good mental therapy. He knew migrating birds around this time often search for just the right landing spots on the numerous water holes dotting the metro and suburban countryside. The warmer the water, the better to rest their wings and perhaps figure out where the hell they're going next.

Temperatures in the Twin Cities that morning began dipping sharply shortly after sunrise, almost as fast as the beaks of the hungry birds on the water dipped for food and the squirrels and gophers foraged among the dead leaves for remains of fallen nuts and apples. The judge, a stocky, broad-shouldered man, although looking somewhat mean, had a gentler side and occasionally smiled as he changed his gaze from the action on the water below to the darkening sky above.

But his frown returned quickly when an airplane burst onto this serene scene. He immediately focused intently on the small blue jet flying south from Twin Cities International Airport, knowing the sight of the plane, privately marked, meant it was time to prepare for a most difficult day.

He then quickly dialed some phone numbers and simply said: "Pelot—all is go." Since Pelot in French Canadian rhymes with go, Sims smiled again, this time over the silly "sing-song" type code. It was almost childish, he thought, despite being involved in this case with an extremely serious and dangerous matter.

Not bothering to shave, the judge dressed quickly, but in his rush to depart for his private swim club—"The Executive Workout"—he nearly forgot to stuff a note with numbers into his gym bag. The note was enclosed in a tough plastic material. He checked the numbers on the note, wrapped it securely around a small but very sharp knife, and then set out on his unusual mission.

However, just before departing he was stopped by the ringing of the phone again. But this time the Caller ID came up with the name "Abbey". Again, there was no indication where the call was coming from. But, like the previous call, he already knew who the caller was and what that person wanted. And this time he did pick up the receiver.

"Abdul!" the voice on the other end said simply.

"Yes," responded the judge impatiently. "The money's coming Abdul. Let your cell know. I've already told you shipments are being made and we have not forgotten you nor the others."

Sims added angrily, "And do not call me again. This can be traced. It is not good for you nor me." With that, he banged the receiver down, put his hat on, straightened his tie and proceeded out the door with a snarl on his face.

The "Land of 10,000 Lakes!" slogan reflecting off the license plates of his Mercedes Benz only added to the judge's frown when his chauffeur opened the car door at 7:45 a.m. for his trip to the swimming pool. After all, Sims thought as he checked out the weather, as a respected judge of one of the great metropolitan areas in the U.S. he should have greater control around him. But he silently scoffed at this wishful thinking, cursing inwardly that it was ridiculous that there was so much water around the whole damn state yet hardly a drop anyone would dare swim in out-doors in October's brisk weather. He had to travel about 30 miles to his club to exercise in surroundings far inferior to the alluring countryside surrounding his home. But the water in his out-door pool was nearly frozen and the size of his pool was certainly no match for his type of strenuous swimming. Besides, his home poolside was still very messy from the night before, when he and some forty of his political allies celebrated around the pool toasting the reappointment of a police chief they were sure they could trust.

The police chief celebration was yet another triumph that could quickly be history as far as Sims was concerned. It was just less weight off his shoulders. But on his trip to the pool he still looked especially burdened, and rightfully so. He was carrying a lot of extra baggage around in the form of worries. For starters, he knew he had a very strange "case" and a great "trial" he was about to face on this day. His case, the gym bag, not only contained the knife and note but also flashy new swim trunks, a trendy jogging outfit, several socks, and two pricey towels enscribed with the gold initials of his club—"EW". He was proud of always being in style. Also tucked away were large goggles, headphones and a flask with his favorite scotch whiskey.

Sims was too much in a hurry to catch a big leisurely breakfast that morning, figuring he could do so at the fancy restaurant nearby his spacious office in downtown St. Paul following his lap swim. Much development in the downtown was due to major financiers in Canada. This was also the case in downtown Minneapolis. He figured the Canadians have loads of money to invest and are willing to spread it around, much as the Japanese were a few years back before their stock market began to plunge.

But he also knew that, like the Asian markets, property investments can go south very quickly. There often is need to look elsewhere besides property and stocks and bonds to maintain and increase wealth, he reasoned. Some will turn to many alternate legitimate methods—but others, in desperation to protect their holdings, may try schemes that border on, or are well into, what could be regarded as illegitimate financial activities.

Whatever the situation, Sims wasn't about to question it. He theorized that his strength as a judge should be able to conquer any accusations of wrongdoing—whether it be in the Bahamas, where birds often chirp instead of shiver and palm trees sway, or in Minnesota where folks mostly wear coats and hats. For some, at least those he often encounters, this may be to cover up what's really going on in the shady depths of their souls, thought Sims.

When the judge arrived at his club's indoor watering hole with his bulging gym bag, even the pool looked rather hostile, unable to be warmed due to absence of sunlight through the large window panes over the pool. Almost at his arrival, raindrops began pattering on the panes sheltering the eight lanes that usually attract more than a dozen avid lap swimmers at this time of the day. With the inclement weather, however, it wasn't surprising that only a few of the bravest swimmers were participating in this morning's "Early Risers" workout.

A part-time lifeguard was on duty, resting on a stool about 10 rungs up while perusing a book. The guard checked his watch and stifled a yawn when noticing the judge, one of the more faithful regulars in the advanced lap group doing his strokes before heading out to their plush, comfy offices.

Since the judge was upset and had very little sleep he was hesitant to encounter the water head-on, which he boastfully claimed he did by diving into it "come hell or high water." He realized, though, that too often the front desk neglected to turn up the thermostat soon enough to beat the arrival of the dedicated lap swimmers when the sun wasn't around. In fact, poolside seemed especially misty and steamy that morning. The little warmth there was seemed to flow from the locker and exercise room. When the judge, still shivering from showering, entered the pool area he was wearing bright red swimming trunks. Although shaking and wet, he appeared unusually trim and muscular for a middle-aged man. The silvery key, which glistened around his neck like a medal, helped to attract attention to his very hairy chest.

At about this time, the guard left his station, hopefully to adjust the thermostat, and Sims got an overview of the large Olympic-sized pool area. There were fewer people there than he had first thought. Most of the usual regulars hadn't even arrived yet, and those doing laps or toweling around the poolside were apparently relatively new members of the exclusive club which Sims belonged to for many years and was regarded as a charter member and founder.

The judge and his cronies placed rigid restrictions on membership. It was sometimes referred to as a "private-private" club. You didn't just join a club like this—you were asked. And those asked, seldom declined the offer—especially if extended by Sims.

The judge didn't feel like diving that morning since the water felt especially cold. He learned long ago that getting his shoulders under water no matter how chilly it might be is basic for reducing shock. Many of the veteran swimmers preferred to shallow dive into the water no matter how frigid. This usually was when the usual lineup of "lappers" following one another allowed such intrusion—and especially when the guard wasn't looking to blow his whistle.

Instead, Sims donned his sporty-looking goggles and simply and quietly submerged when he thought he spotted the person he was looking for, although at this point every face seemed somewhat identical. All wore goggles, which for many further distorted their faces.

As he began rapidly swimming in lane 5 the person he spotted was watching him through the mist and made a very smooth and graceful dive into the water from the opposite end of lane six.

As usual, the pool water was rather murky, not having been cleaned properly prior to the swimmers' arrival. Sims had expressed his disappointment in the maintaining of the pool earlier in the week. However, with the help of his special goggles, he could clearly identify the form of the other swimmer rapidly approaching him under water like a sleek sea creature bent on swallowing prey while speeding through the glistening haze in the next lane. The two swam, head down, stroking arms in Olympic fashion while keeping their kicking legs closely together to cut a quick and straight path to one another without causing many ripples.

While all this was going on, the lifeguard was approaching the club's reception desk. Lillian Norton, the club receptionist who helped unlock the club doors in the morning, was just opening the cash register and looking through her paper work. She seemed surprised to see the young guard, Roger Moore, one of the member's college-aged sons working during the school year to help pay for his wild spring breaks.

She could only shrug her shoulders when the guard asked where the maintenance man could be located. Her retort was simply, "If you're looking for Martin Sloan…who knows? All I know is there's lots of cold people wanting to yell at him. He's tough to find this morning." The guard persisted, "But he left a note. He wants to see me…something about the thermostat. The water's real chilly out there and I've got to be back for my next swim session in a few minutes."

Lillian sighed, saying with far less sarcasm: "Well what do you know. Here's a note Sloan left for me…it says you're to see him in the boiler room right now." She then demanded, "and when you're there, tell him I need to see him after he's through with whatever it is he's doing."

The hallway leading to the boiler plant resembles a dark tunnel. For some reason not fully explained, the architect forgot to install any windows. Without proper lighting Roger had difficulty trying to spot the head janitor from a distance.

"That you Martin?" he hollered—his voice almost creating an echo down the hall.

"Sure is kid. I thought you'd be here earlier," Sloan yelled back in his usual tough manner. "I need some help trying to warm up the pool. Suppose by now those big shots are complaining. Bunch of phonies, I've probably got more cash than many of them."

"No—but they will be if I don't hurry up and get back," said Roger annoyed and glancing at his watch. He had only a few minutes to get ready for the next swim group—called the intermediate lappers. And he also had to do some studying for a school exam later in the day. "Yeah, okay, see if you can help me loosen this faucet, it seems to be stuck," the janitor asked with a growl. The teenage lifeguard didn't know anything about plumbing but it was obvious Sloan had a problem. He picked up one of the pipe wrenches nearby to make the janitor happy.

However, with just a slight tug on the wrench it easily turned the faucet, much to the guard's surprise. "Aw, you're just weak Marty," Roger said teasingly, flexing an arm muscle as though he was Minnesota's wrestler-turned-governor.

The janitor failed to see the humor, however, and in an almost angered tone of voice said, "You goddam young punks—half of you are on steroids. Most of you are full of drugs and wanting more. Believe me, I know all about your kind."

Somewhat taken back by this sudden mad outburst, Roger checked his watch to make a fast exit, but Sloan remembered he had one more job for him. "I know you have to go, but just give me a lift with some of these pool cleaning cartons. I've been meaning to get them out of my way since we had an extra delivery about a week ago. It won't take long." The young man shrugged, grabbed hold of one end of each carton and helped carry them to a shelf nearby. But before the last carton was carried, Roger got more nervous about extending his stay too long. "This has to be the last, Marty, I really have to get back or I'm on the shit list around here." Sloan replied with a smirk, "Sure kid, I know what you mean, that Lillian can be real mean." After tossing up the final carton, the guard went quickly on his way, almost forgetting to tell the janitor that Lillian wanted to see him.

The walk back seemed even longer than the trip to the boiler room for the anxious lifeguard. But he knew this was because he was so late in returning. When he finally arrived at the doors leading to the pool, he listened for any voices or splashing of water before entering. Everything was silent, however, so he wasn't surprised to see that most of the busy executives had left and were most likely still showering before departing in their expensive cars and tooling downtown.

Roger knew the regular lap swimmers were aware that the lifeguards, especially the part-time college kids, had to come and go at times when homework demanded and didn't wish to be around when the next swimming classes began. All he had to do now was to clean up after the regulars—removing the towels and checking for any items they may have left behind.

As he walked around poolside, the young lifeguard stopped at the far left corner lane and decided that with any luck Sloan may have had a chance to get the water at least to a comfortable temperature by now. With that, he put his foot into the water but found it to be nearly as cold as it was before fixing the thermostat. "That goofball janitor," muttered Roger.

It was when he looked up disgruntled to check the wall clock that his eyes caught something on the bottom of the far left lane. At first it seemed to be just a pile of towels. But he looked again—it was more like a form of some kind. Thinking that damn chemical treatment of Sloan's was clouding his vision, he walked closer to the corner to make out what this actually was—probably something a swimmer forgot.

But upon peering farther down into the water, he could see that it was a shape that looked more like a human body. It was all curled up and wasn't moving. With this in mind, he stirred the water with his foot to look more intensely. Damn—it sure was a body! It was Judge Sims at the bottom of the pool in a crouched, almost fetal-like position.

Once the excited lifeguard sounded the alarm it was only a matter of minutes that the paramedics arrived and attempted to breathe life into the limp body of Sims. However, after about 30 minutes, all rescuers agreed that Sims indeed was dead. The judge became another statistic— a drowning victim at age 53.

CHAPTER 2

Al Benjamin never quite made it to city editor. He was told he had a great nose for news, but his managerial skills left lots to be desired. His eyes weren't so bad either. There were very few mistakes that ever got by him as he read newspaper proof for the early edition. If Benjamin was on the copy desk of the morning paper, the city desk felt more assured that the final edition would be near letter perfect.

His eyes skirted about on the proof sheets while his mind focused mostly on strolling through corn stalks ready to catch a pheasant or two in his sights. He was proofing page 3 when he noticed the story brought in for the first run by the rookie city hall reporter on the reported Sims drowning.

Since he knew Sims from childhood days, he read the story word for word instead of just checking it out for typos. In fact, he used his office magnifying glass to make sure it was okay.

His first reaction was that the reporter did a lousy job. The judge was a great swimmer. Benjamin went to high school with Sims and remembered him as being captain of the swim team. So, he reasoned, the judge must have had a fatal heart attack or something like that. But, he also recalled, Sims was in such fine shape that he could often be found pumping iron and jogging with the young jocks when he wasn't swimming laps.

However, the newspaper account simply stated that he drowned—no cramps, no seizure, nothing. At this point Benjamin realized he was getting tired. The clock nearby pointed to 1 a.m. Benjamin hated the damn night shift, which he had been on and off of since joining the Tribune 20 years ago. In thinking about the time, he also was aware that the city hall reporter probably had no time to check with the examining mortician as to the exact cause of drowning. He knew, too, that an autopsy had to be done and that the reporter would file a followup story Monday morning giving more details. But then he suddenly remembered that he was given the assignment to fill in on the city hall beat Monday. "Oh God, hunting time is all screwed up…there's only about 10 hours tomorrow to get the limit," he said to himself sighing.

Sunday turned out to be a big disappointment for Benjamin. Most of the time he and his companions were in a car going to and coming from the hunting site on a friend's farm near the border of Iowa looking for birds. In fact, they only were able to bag three apiece—with most being shot from their car while driving along a country road. You might say, the highlight of the whole day was going to church before taking off for the hunting trip. At least he saw Alice Crimmons again, who was always giving him her negative views following services about city hall where she worked.

His wife Kay didn't seem to care too much about his hunting disappointments. One thing she really despised was having to clean the dead fowl. They often had all kind of shot left in them. Benjamin wasn't a great shooter, and he hardly ever ate the ones he bagged. That night Al, tired and disgruntled as he was over the hunt, took a moment to jot a reminder to himself to go to city hall first thing in the morning rather than to the newspaper office to start his reporting duties for the day.

On Monday, city hall at 8 a.m. is just waking up in Minneapolis. In fact, Benjamin had to wait a half hour talking to a bailiff before permitted to enter the department where news of public record was filed. He read the sketchy drowning report compiled by police as well as their other reports of happenings making news on the day of the drowning.

He scratched down some notes, and then looked for more details not found in Saturday night's first run.

It didn't take long to realize the reporter did a lazy as well as lousy job. He was in one hell of a hurry. He wasn't at the scene and just simply rewrote the brief police report, Al concluded. "But my God, an important judge—a prominent and controversial person like Sims, a man so well known around the state who did so much, should have at least rated a good major spot on the front page and not just a mention in the makeup section.," Benjamin muttered to himself while scratching his bald head in frustration.

During his time on the Trib Al covered every beat. That's why he had no trouble calling on the chief medical examiner's office near city hall. But things were different now. A reporter didn't get as much respect. He had to sign in and was told Dr. John Loring, M.E. was too busy to see him until the next day. Remembering an old newspaper trick, Al went out to the hall and found a phone. He placed a handkerchief over the speaker to disguise his voice and then told the secretary screening calls that this was an emergency.

After many minutes, Loring answered."What can I do for you?" he asked gruffly.

"Doc, this is Al Benjamin from the Tribune. My editor's wondering what really happened to Judge Sims?" Loring growled back, "He drowned, can't you read"

"I didn't read enough. What did the autopsy find?" "The report said no one was there when it happened. That means you gotta do an autopsy, right?" The more cantankerous Loring became the more Al kept prying. He waited for either the phone to click off or the arrogant coroner to think up a reply. Fortunately it was the latter.

"We don't have the body in the forensic lab…it's in cold storage waiting for the funeral. What do you want me to do…interrupt the funeral?"

Benjamin wasn't to be denied. "The story said the funeral isn't until tomorrow. Seems you still have time to check things out."

"You want to go to the funeral home to look over my shoulder?" Loring snorted.

He was surprised when Al responded quickly, "Sure, tell me when and where."

"I'm too busy for guys like you Benjamin," the coroner bellowed, almost loosing control. After a long pause and apparently regaining his composure somewhat, he added, "Okay, meet my assistant Dr. DeSantro over at our lab at about 3 p.m. He'll have a report. What are you snooping around for anyway?"

"I'll be there," is all Benjamin could say, after moving away from the loud, irritating voice and hanging up.

Doctor Ramon DeSantro was an exact opposite of Dr. Loring. A native of Central America, he grew up amid poverty and terrorism and took his medical training by bits and pieces in various schools around Colombia with missionary help before interning at Minneapolis General. He reflected patience and a little humility—something sorely needed by his boss.

Upon arriving at the ME lab, Al was told by DeSantro that he had already examined the body as soon as notified by Loring. However, Benjamin noted that autopsy tools were still on the shelf as though unused.

"You've got everyone mad at you," warned DeSantro. "Loring is really pissed. It wasn't easy to notify the Sims family of this. And the funeral director is angry that we're so late."

"Sorry—but Frank Sims was an expert swimmer. He wasn't a drowner," responded the middle-aged journalist.

"He also had a heart seizure brought on by what appears to be muscle spasm," interrupted DeSantro. "Your man must have been terribly out of shape. The entire muscle wall caved in around the heart," the doctor noted.

'I'm surprised, Sims was an athlete. He could have competed for a gold medal," Al said.

"Did you find anything out of the ordinary?"

"Not really. It's just a drowning Benjamin." With that, the annoyed DeSantro looked again at his report.

He then added, "But Sims apparently wasn't quite the athlete you believed. Looks like he was a diabetic. He had a tiny fresh needle mark on the upper thigh. He must have had his morning's insulin before diving in."

Benjamin shrugged, "I'm sure it didn't run in the family—his folks seemed so hardy."

"Doesn't mean a thing, it may have come from his grandmother," shrugged DeSantro. "But he may have gotten it recently, a type two. However, I didn't notice any more marks. But then again I wasn't looking for diabetes."

CHAPTER 3

The reporter still had DeSantro's words in mind about diabetes when he returned to his word processor at the newspaper office to file his followup story.

But before he did, he thought he'd contact Sims' brother Jack to check out the judge's health. He also knew Jack from years ago and recalled he was a pretty nice guy compared to his brother who often talked down to people outside of his influential circle of lawyers and bankers.

"Jack—Al Benjamin from the Trib. So sorry to hear about Frank," was his opener on the phone with Sims' brother. "I'm doing a followup obituary, and wanted to personally extend my sympathy. I remember Frank so well in school—what a great athlete.

"Imagine you're shocked that he was a drowning victim—he appeared to be in superb shape." Pausing, he then asked, "Was Frank in poor health lately?"

The response was hesitant. "Oh yeah—Al. Thanks. It was quite a shock. As far as I know, Frank just had a complete checkup recently and was very healthy. He was always into physical fitness, you know. Suppose it was just his time."

"The medical examiner said he may have had diabetes. Were you aware of that?" Benjamin asked.

"No—not Frank. He went to the same doctor I go to, Tom Samuelson, who told me just the other day I should try to be as healthy as my brother. He said Frank was a perfect specimen—he didn't have to be on medicine of any kind."

As usual Al was taking notes and felt he learned enough. After again offering condolences, he hung up—but kept wondering why the judge had a needle mark in his leg. His first inclination was to talk to Dr. Samuelson. But before he could dial, his phone rang. It was Alice, who wondered if he had heard about Frank Sims.

"The whole thing stinks," she declared. "It all fits in to what I've been telling you."

Benjamin thought he must have missed something. "What do you mean, Alice?"

"That drug ring I mentioned to you. That judge was part of that entire mess."

Alice told him so many things off and on over the years that the reporter had a difficult time making any sense out of this conversation. However, he did recall she was talking to him once about drugs and some of the underworld figures her ex-husband knew. He could never figure out why such an apparent nice lady as Alice got tied up with such a shady ass as Zack Crimmons.

"Whoa!—back up Alice! I'm not following this."

"Remember, I told you some of our top lawyers and bankers were in on this…Sims must have had a falling out with some of them. Why else would they kill him?"

"Time out, Alice! Who killed who?" Benjamin knew this was poor grammar, but he also knew you had to get your words in fast, rightly or wrongly, to carry on a conversation with Alice. For some reason, she chose him as a sounding board for some of her frustrations. Many in the media thought she was a joke, but Al had mixed feelings. He took a little time with her. She wasn't wrong about her former husband—he was truly a bastard. But, what Benjamin couldn't figure out, was why hadn't someone put a cork in Alice's mouth a long time ago?

He hadn't known Alice when she was a co-called swinger with Crimmons. He only knew the split with him left her and her two identical twin daughters with a big expensive home in the Heights along with a mortgage but little else. Moreover, she whispered to Benjamin that her ex husband had threatened to take everything from her and turn her into a penniless prostitute if she ever left him.

Instead, she apparently turned to religion to cope with her frustrations and hostilities. Alice was now very active in church affairs. When she wasn't serving on the church council she was a lay distributor. She met Al when he was on the council and began talking with him about her experiences and views when she found out he was a reporter, and whenever their paths seemed to cross.

Benjamin had to confess that he also tried to avoid Alice when he was in a hurry. Like others, he was sure, the jury was "still out" on her stability and on what effect Zack and his ugly associates really had on her mind. But, basically, she seemed to be a very good person—and to have it all together at times. It's just that when she opened her mouth, instead of what one would expect to hear from a frequent churchgoer—all this knowledge and rage about vice poured out. And the question always arose: what's fact or fiction with Alice?

Just then the reporter was beeped on his cell phone that another call was on the line. "Alice, I have another caller—let's finish this up at lunch tomorrow." Since he planned to attend Sims' wake downtown later in the afternoon he suggested they meet at Toby's restaurant, a few blocks from the funeral home.

The other call was from Doctor DeSantro.

"Mr. Benjamin, I thought you'd like to know that I did discover something else while checking over the Sims' body. There were some numbers tattooed between his toes…just a bunch of tiny numbers, like a brand."

Al winced, "geez—that must have hurt like hell."

Following a long pause, DeSantro said, "I mentioned this to his wife. It would have nothing to do with his death, of course, but I thought you might be interested for some reason."

"Thanks, did she already know about it?"

"Apparently she did. Said he was into tattoos—but I didn't see any others on him."

"But why between the toes?—that's sure a poor place for anyone to admire them," Al commented. "What are the numbers?"

"They're very difficult to make out…so small-between the fourth and fifth toes on the left foot. See them at the lab if you want—but I have to run now." Since Benjamin planned to meet Alice at noon the next day, he arranged for a meeting with DeSantro at mid morning so he'd have plenty of time to get to the restaurant. But the next morning didn't go quite as planned. For one thing, Al had to wait about an hour for DeSantro. When he did come, the doc seemed very nervous—looking at his watch as though he had somewhere else to rush off to.

In fact, before Al could even say hello, DeSantro, nattily attired in a loud sport coat instead of his usual conservative white smock, quickly told him the bad news—the judge was cremated overnight. "Believe me, Mr. Benjamin—I just found out myself. Doctor Loring said the widow changed her mind and instead wanted the remains cremated immediately."

"But what about those numbers? You wanted me to see them. How the hell can someone just go off and destroy a body without knowing what exactly caused death? It's still a mystery to me." DeSantro responded aloofly, "Mr. Benjamin, I said he drowned. As for the numbers, I'm sure the widow knows them. They may just be some marks from his military service."

"On his toes?—he must have been a pretty tough Marine," scoffed Al. "And tell me—why would he have a needle puncture if he wasn't diabetic—or even on drugs?"

DeSantro, losing patience, arose from his chair as though to leave, but reconsidered and sat down, removed his glasses as if in deep thought, and said: "How do you know he wasn't on insulin?"

"Cause his brother would have told me…and the family physician said he wasn't on it. Suppose he got scratched in the pool?"

"No, it was definitely from a needle. However, the muscles around the wound as well as much of the body were different."

"What do you mean—different?"

"They seemed more atrophied, much more contracted than they should be…even with rigor mortis setting in."

"What would cause that?" asked Al. DeSantro shrugged, "I'm not sure. The only similar cases I've seen were in Bogota. Some of the drugs used over there could tighten up the muscles until they snapped. In a way they can be related to potassium chloride mixed with pain and nerve deadening stimulant. In fact, some were often injected for torture or execution in prison compounds."

"Could that be given by a needle?" asked Benjamin. "Yes, that's how most of them were administered," said the doctor.

"Could Sims swim if he had that in him?"

"He'd go into seizure in a few seconds and sink like a rock," remarked DeSantro in thinking of how slim the chances would be. Al, wondering how so much could be known by a guy that probably didn't even open up the body, then asked, "would he appear to have the same thing as cramps?"

"An acute case. He'd loose consciousness immediately. There's usually no traces of it in the bloodstream. I must go now. By the way, there will be a memorial service the widow said."

"Sure Doc. Thanks for the time. I have to rush, too…I've gotta date with a lady."

CHAPTER 4

By the time Al arrived at Toby's he was already at least 15 minutes late. However, there was no big hurry since Alice was nowhere around. He asked for a table facing the door so she'd spot him right away. However, after 45 minutes went by the reporter had sipped enough coffee and read the morning paper at least twice. He was getting a bit upset since he had to get back to work but still wanted to stop off at the Sims' service.

After 15 more minutes of waiting he decided to order and rapidly digested some lukewarm soup and a sandwich. Each time the restaurant door opened, he looked to see if the person entering was Alice. Upon finishing off a piece of pie, which he ordered just to kill time, and consuming some more bitter coffee he once again checked his watch and then decided it was time to leave.

Alice didn't seem to be the type to stand you up. He met with her several times in the past and she had always been very punctual. But he knew she usually had lots on her mind and that something came up. Although he could understand all this, he still wondered why she at least didn't call the restaurant and try to page him.

Rain and road repair work also delayed him on the way to the mortuary. When he arrived, he could hardly find a parking space because of all the vehicles parked at the funeral home and many blocks around it. "By God, it must be great to be so popular even when you die," muttered Benjamin as he circled the large funeral home twice. He realized Sims was well known and the type cars around the mortuary made it quite apparent that most of his friends were very affluent and just plain rich. Parking his old jalopy next to a shiny new Porsche convertible helped to give Al that extra humility needed to enter the funeral home with head bowed.

Inside the mortuary, he checked his umbrella and looked around for some old faces he thought he might know from his school days. He could spot a few, even though many were adorned with beards and specs. However, most were known to him only from his reading the newspapers—some were prominent lawyers and bankers and others were also important looking gents with expensive suits who probably knew the judge through business or legal matters.

Apparently Mrs. Sims did a good job in letting them know about the memorial service. It seemed strange there was no casket to say a few prayers for the recently departed, as is the custom of Roman Catholics. He couldn't help but think this was more like a social event with so many grouped together chatting about everything but the deceased. Even the widow seemed to be smiling and laughing too much.

Instead of a body to view, there were numerous photos of the judge growing up, in the service, and as a college and law student. None showed Sims as a judge, which caused Al to wonder. At that point he felt a firm hand on his shoulder. He saw that it was connected to the arm of what appeared to be Andy Sapel, president of Sapel Realty and Gas Co.,a snobby rich kid who ran the 4:40 with Al in high school.Andy usually won, but not always fair and square,and whatever it took.

"Shocking isn't it Al?" remarked Sapel rather insincerely. Sapel grew a beard since the reporter saw him last. It made him look even more sleazy, Al thought. His eyes were still icy cold though.

"You knew him well, like I did. Such a great guy and such a sudden ending. All the good ones seem to go fast they say."

Al almost bit his tongue when thinking if that's so Sapel should live a very, very long life. Instead, he said simply, "too bad there aren't any recent photos of him—when he looked so darn healthy."

"Yeah—well you never know when your time's up do we? I understand though he had diabetes so bad it led to a heart attack under water."

The reporter stared Sapel in the eyes with that remark. There was nothing reported about a heart attack He wondered if he was getting his facts straight—but then spotted Sim's brother Jack who had told him the judge never had diabetes.

"The authorities aren't sure yet how he died Andy," Al noted. He knew this wasn't the time nor the place to argue about this. He also had to leave, his city editor wanted stories he picked up on his beat. Signing the register, he was amazed at the many signatures of presidents and CEOs. Some were from major corporations around town—people with exceptional influence. People, he figured, with so much power they could tell you when to speak and when to shut up.

Upon returning to his cluttered desk at the Trib, Benjamin immediately saw the note near his word processor. Scrawled by another reporter, it read: "Plz call wife—very important."

Calling Kay in late afternoon usually was an exercise in futility. That was the time she'd either be on the phone with her sister or out shopping or visiting the daughter. But strangely enough, this time she was at the phone after only a few rings.

"You called?" asked Benjamin, a man of a few words when communicating with home.

"Yes—weren't you going to see Alice Crimmons this noon?"

"Yep—she stood me up."

"No she didn't. She's dead…a suicide. Her body was found in her garage this morning. I heard about it on the radio. I suppose it'll be in the evening paper."

CHAPTER 5

Kay was right. There was a brief story ready to be filed on the desk of Joe Thorne, the regular police reporter. It simply stated the facts: Alice G. Crimmons, 501 Riverview Heights, former wife of Attorney Zachoria Crimmons, was found dead in her parked car this morning, apparently from asphyxiation. The body was discovered in her closed garage by a neighbor. Crimmons was a former school teacher at Riverview Heights elementary and active in church organizations. She is survived by two daughters, Sarah and Susan.

Benjamin read the writeup twice to make sure this was the same Alice Crimmons he had just talked to yesterday. She must have been starting the car to meet him at the restaurant. He was especially puzzled by the fact that Alice didn't seem depressed at all when he was chatting with her last. She was so pleasant and ready to gossip…a determined little thing, bent on making things right.

He cornered Thorne at the coffee machine to find out more details. But the police snoop confirmed that it looked like just another self-planned tragedy. He did mention, however, that an autopsy was being done.

It took only a few minutes for Benjamin to be on the phone once again with the Medical Examiner's office. Only this time he knew specifically the guy to ask for.

Unfortunately, however, Doctor DeSantro was out of town. Instead, he was referred to the ME.'s other assistant, Dr. Arthur Erickson, who told Al he performed the autopsy in the absence.of DeSantro who had to rush back to Central America for a visit with his parents.

He was also reassured by Erickson that Alice's death was simply caused by inhaling too many fumes from the exhaust of a car.

"In other words, she simply did herself in," concluded Erickson.

"You found nothing different at all, Doc? No details at all out of the ordinary? I knew this fine lady and she just wouldn't think of taking her own life"

"Lots of times they can fool you," Erickson reminded."She looked okay otherwise. However, I must say she had a terrible pained expression on her face. Could be she was in shock from diabetes and didn't realize the car was running?"

"Why do you say that?"

"Well, I noticed what appears to be a tiny needle mark on her leg which could indicate she was on insulin." Since there was a long pause the doctor wondered if Benjamin was still on the phone. "hello, hello— you still there Al?"

"Yeah—thanks doc. I guess I've heard enough. Oh, by the way…when do you expect Doc DeSantro to get back?"

"In about three weeks I understand, if he finds everything okay down there."

Diabetes seemed to be on a rampage, thought Benjamin on hanging up. There was no way of knowing if Alice actually had the disease except by contacting her doctor, and he didn't want to do that. But he suddenly thought of another way. As he recalled, his nephew Joey the cop had been dating one of Alice's daughters. Besides, the thought had also occurred to him that this might be an excellent time for him to chat with Joe a little about what's been going on.

Still considering what to do, Benjamin finished off some of his stories for the morning run and went home. It was still raining as he propped his feet on his favorite ottoman and enjoyed some really good coffee while waiting for Kay to come home. She had a note on the kitchen table saying she was out grocery shopping. But Al knew she probably also stopped off at many other stores on the way.

Not wanting to break with his tradition, he tuned in on the evening TV news which rehashed most of the major stories he already had perused in the Trib a few hours earlier. There was no mention of Alice's demise, of course, since everyone at the paper seemed convinced it was just another suicide and could wait for tomorrow's regular obituary section.

As Benjamin got up to refill his coffee, however, a new story caught his eye. He was surprised to see the face of Dr. Raymon DeSantro peering in to his living room from the TV screen. He was so surprised, in fact, that he almost missed the newscaster's remarks that DeSantro was among those believed to be on a small plane that crashed near the Bahamas early in the day.

The question of why he was in the Bahamas flashed in the reporter's mind since he recalled that doc Erickson said DeSantro was back home visiting—in Central America. It was about this time that Al also heard the back door open as Kay brought in the groceries, and other parcels. After her usual, "yoo hoo! I'm home," he sat back in his chair and wondered if he was in for any more shocking news before the day was through.

As a veteran reporter, he only briefly mentioned events of his work to his wife. Sometimes it was best not to go into too many details or suspicions-for the sake of the teller as well as the listener. He learned long ago, that until things are "off the press" and not "off the record" it may not be wise to talk too freely.

After dinner, he did ask Kay, however, if she had been in touch with her sister's bachelor son Joey recently. She said he'd been on vacation lately and his parents were a bit upset that they hadn't heard from him while he was gone.

"They just don't realize that he's a full-grown man now," shrugged Kay.

"Yeah, I understand the kid's a swinger. But even though he is your sister's kid, I've always liked him. You can count on him-you can trust him," Al noted.

CHAPTER 6

Joseph D. Kavinski was just finishing up another report when he got a call from his uncle Al. It was about 10 a.m. and the young police lieutenant was thinking about getting another cup of coffee to help wake him up from the night before when the phone rang.

Joe heard more from his uncle than he did from his aunt Kay, mostly because they both had so many similar interests—especially when it came to hunting and fishing.

"Heard you were on vacation Joe—get any birds?"

"Nope—this time I was hunting for women—otherwise known to you chauvinistic middle-aged bird lovers as 'chicks', uncle Al," responded the cop.

"Well, I hope you were more successful than you are in catching pheasants," said Al. Lighting a cigarette and glancing at all the back paper work on his desk, Kavinsky asked, "What's up?" Like his reporter uncle, he minced words and made small talk only so far.

"Let's do lunch. I might have some information for you-relating to Sims and Alice Crimmons. You're still dating Suzy Crimmons aren't you?" His nephew corrected him, "Sarah—unc, Sarah. I know they look alike, but as an expert I know one from the other. God, I was stunned when I heard about their mom. That's hard to figure. As for the judge, I just got a report from his widow."

"Yeah, what's it say?" asked Benjamin "She had her home broken into," said Joe. "It was ramsacked. Damn—you'd think they could leave a widow alone in her grief. Believe, me, unc, if you knew the assholes I have to check out in this business…"

"Well, maybe I can help. At least it's worth a try. Where's your favorite watering hole?" asked Al. "Unlike reporters unc, I don't drink on duty. And it sounds like you may have me on duty. Besides, I have one hell of a hangover. But I'll meet you at noon at Maxy's cause I know that's where you like to watch the models strut their stuff."

Benjamin was proud of his nephew. Only 34, the kid already had an impressive arrests record in homicide. He caught on quickly and his confidence could fill a room even before entering it.

His uncle was already sipping on a beer when Joe arrived.

"Where's all the lingerie, unc?," joked the young detective as he sat down at the small corner table. He referred to the sleeky store models who often showed off their slinkiest apparel around the male guests at lunch.

"Joe, you're going to be the death of your mother if you don't stop running after the broads and dodging bullets."

"Aw—you're no fun. Besides, I'm a straight arrow now. I'm spending most of my time dating decent women—like Sarah Crimmons."

Benjamin was glad for the opening. He asked his nephew if Sarah ever mentioned any of her mom's eccentricities. "Only that she was scared stiff about her ex," said Joe.

"She told the girls some weird stories about their dad and how he promised to ruin her—make her a whore—if she left him."

"Did you think she was a flake?"

"Only time will tell. I think she was a nice lady but married to a real s.o.b."

"Do you figure he had anything to do with her death?," the reporter questioned, his suspicions aroused.

"I was told it just a suicide, plain and simple."

"By whom?," asked Al. "By Loring, the head medical examiner," Joe replied.

"He has to—it's legally required".

"Not for Loring it ain't. I had to really push him for one on Sims and I still don't think it was done. His wife cremated him before questions were asked. Did Alice's doc find anything suspicious?"

"He didn't indicate anything," said Joe taking a cigarette from his pocket. Benjamin couldn't help but notice the gun on his nephew's belt when Joe's outdated sport jacket spread open while putting the cigarette to his mouth.

"You've got to get rid of that habit, Joey, or the nicotine's gonna kill you before a bullet."

"Too late, unc, I'm hooked. Besides, it's my only vice, just ask Sarah."

"Okay, but how about you asking her if her ma ever had diabetes? Loring didn't do the autopsy—his associate Erickson did and he said he spotted a needle mark. It's like one for insulin, only longer and leaves a more definite small mark on the skin according to Erickson."

"You've been doing some snooping again, haven't you unc? What else do you know about all this?"

With that, Benjamin began telling his eye-roving nephew about the similar needle mark on Sims' body, the numbers between the toes, Alice's suspicion's about her husband's underworld connections, and, finally, Dr. DeSantro's sudden death around the Bahamas—when he should have been elsewhere. He was interrupted only by the waitress when she brought the soup and by models who seemed to go out of their way to distract his smiling young companion.

Joe put out his cigarette and looked at his soup. "I guess I heard a little about Zack's criminal ties from Sarah, unc, but the rest is all news. She's never ever mentioned that her mom was on insulin, by the way. I'll do some checking. Have you mentioned any of this to anyone else?…to aunt Kay or anyone?"

"You're the only one so far. I never tell Kay anything, you know how these women blab."

Joe chuckled. "Damn—you sure are a chauvinist. Good she shouldn't know—for her own sake. What you're telling me could be very explosive. Lots of people could be involved, even the guy next door. Just sit on it now, unc, and let me take over for awhile. Could be drugs."

After sipping his soup and peeking at a passing blonde in a two-piece swimsuit, he looked at his uncle and said, "And I think I'll begin with a dip in the pool tomorrow morning.

It's a cinch I need the exercise. I've been wanting to get active at that club ever since joining it a few months ago. It was tough to get a membership—sure is snooty. Judge Sims and his group must have been black-balling me."

"You're still into martial arts, aren't you?" asked Benjamin, recalling that his nephew always was a good scrapper even as a kid around the neighborhood.

"To survive, unc. And since swimmng's better for the circulation, I'll circulate around the pool for openers."

CHAPTER 7

Although getting up at 5 a.m. wasn't exactly his style, Kavinsky managed to drag himself out the door and to the health club, taking his shaver and tooth brush with him. He hardly remembered where the locker was once he checked in at the reception desk. In fact, he considered himself lucky to still have a card to stick into the computer ID membership machine allowing him to enter.

Joe used to know a few club members, but he realized none of his friends would be dumb enough to be up this early for a plunge in cold water. Although the sun was peeking in through the panes, he shuddered at the mere thought of being near the pool.

He was right. There was no one he knew. They all seemed to be middle-aged or older except the few women doing their laps. About the only youthful face belonged to the guy perched on the lifeguard seat half awake. He wondered if this could be the same guard on duty the morning of the Sims incident.

Upon removing his towel from around his stocky shoulders, Kavinsky wandered over to the foot of the lifeguard ladder. Looking up, he found the young man's eyes almost closed.

"Hello—we keeping you up?" he asked with his cockeyed grin.

Somewhat startled, the guard peered down at his inquisitor. Seeing a younger man around this place at this time was rather surprising in itself. Not knowing quite what to say, and a bit embarrassed about his sleepy condition, he simply smiled back.

"I'm Joe Kavinsky…how about you?"

The guard almost fumbled for his name. "Roger—Roger Moore. You must be new around here."

"I've been a member the past several months…mostly for racquetball. This is the first time swimming—so keep an eye on me." Again came the slight smile. With the guard more comfortable,

Joe asked if he's always on duty for the early swim. The guard replied the only exception was on weekends and Mondays and Fridays due to his school schedule.

Acknowledging this was a lot of time for a student, Joe joked that this must cut into his love life. The guard kidded back saying this sure wasn't the place to find a lover, although noting there were some sharp-looking gals around now with the more flexible club rules.

"Suppose you were here when Judge Sims drowned?" Kavinsky asked, taking advantage of the friendly conversation.

The smile began to fade from the college student's face. "I try to forget that day," he said looking away.

"Yeah, I'll bet you do. I read about it. Not many details though. What lane did it happen in?," asked Joe, who tried to be as casual as possible without turning the young man off.

"I found the body near the corner of lane 6, near the edge of the pool."

"Do you know where he entered the water?"

"No…that was the time I was gone," admitted the lifeguard. Embarrassed, he explained, "I was asked to help our janitor in the boiler room heat the water in the pool for a short time."

Noting his embarrassment, Kavinsky tried to change the subject somewhat. "Well, I gotta be getting back to work soon Guess I'll do some laps. Is it okay to dive in where you can?"

"Sure I'll let you. We usually only allow it when there's a break in the swimming lanes." When Joe took the plunge he wondered if Sims dove in from the same location. He kept this in mind as he tried to keep up with the experienced lappers who pressed him from all directions, bent on getting in the number of laps they were committed to…come hell or high water.

Not having swam for some time, Kavinsky struggled around the lanes and was surprised at how long it seemed to swim from one lane to another. The water was relatively clear despite recent chlorination and Joe could easily see swimmers coming and going as he put his head down between strokes.

When he finally completed several.lanes he was almost gasping. Reaching for the pool steps, he grabbed onto them and began climbing up when he noticed feet—they belonged to Roger Moore.

"Man, I thought I was gonna have to yell for your help. I didn't realize I was in such poor shape," Joe said panting as he wondered why the guard was there to greet him.

"I thought you might want to see where I found Mr. Sims," the guard remarked without smiling. He added, "I figured you must be asking for some reasons."

"I'm sure you've gone through it all many times," said Joe as he put a towel around his shoulder to both dry off and warm up. "I'm Joe Kavinsky from the police department, but I'm not on official duty so please don't think I'm badgering you about this." He quickly added, "It's all gone down as a drowning—and you haven't been implicated in any way."

Smiling, the guard replied, as if in relief: "Yeah, I know. Here's where I found the judge," he said pointing to the bottom of the pool near the lower corner of the lane 6. "He was all hunched up…like he had a terrible case of cramps. There was nothing no one could do."

Looking back at Joe, he added, "I figured you might be an insurance inspector or something…but not a cop."

"I'm just curious is all," Joe said nonchalantly to put the guard more at ease.

Pointing to his life guard perch, Roger explained, "It was tough to get a good look at the entire pool from where I sit. The sun wasn't shining and it was kinda misty around poolside. Martin Sloan, the janitor, just put some stuff in the water that clouded it up somewhat, too," the guard recalled.

"Could you see many you knew the morning of the accident?" Joe thought this was a good time to get some more questions in with the guard starting to get chatty with him again. "Are there any that stand out in your mind?"

"Matter of fact, I didn't. There weren't many using the pool that morning...must have been the bad weather. The judge was about the only one I recognized from up there," said the guard pointing again to his perch. "But I do remember there were even a few women swimmers. That's unusual, this group is usually always all men."

"Did you notice anything different about the judge?"

The guard paused, then chuckled, "Everybody looks alike with those darn goggles. There were ladies diving and the judge was wearing some jazzy swim trunks and had that big key around his neck."

"A key...what kind of a key?" asked Joe.

"Probably just a locker key. But bigger than our locker keys."

"Did the paramedics take it off—or where did it go?"

"No, by gosh, it wasn't on the judge when they were there. It must have fallen off."

Kavinsky checked his water-proof watch. "Well thanks. Nice meeting you Roger. Oh, by the way—did you say Martin Sloan is the janitor?"

"Yeah, why?" asked the guard. "Oh nothing...I notice he's missed a few spots."

CHAPTER 8

Soon after he arrived at his precinct, Kavinsky began checking the files for any info on a Martin Sloan. He recalled that name from somewhere but wasn't sure from what source. Usually when a name attracted him he could find it in the police files.

"Hey Charlie…ever book a Sloan?"

His question was directed at Charles McKay of the narcotics squad who was passing by. McKay usually knew as much about drug pushers as anyone around town. In fact, he once worked for the cops as an inside man in a drug-trafficking syndicate and almost got blown away when he was discovered just before police burst in to break up a major cocaine exchange with a group from the Bahamas.

"Sloan…Sloan," McKay muttered as he walked toward Kavinsky. "Seems to me there was a Sloan caught in a bust about two years ago on Hennepin Avenue. He was a fat little bastard…one of Leo Anthony's creeps if I'm not mistaken.

"Why, have you run into him?"

With the mention of Anthony's name, Joe looked up from checking the files. Anthony had been put in the slammer a few years back for running one of the biggest cocaine chains in the nation, perhaps internationally.

"Maybe. Was his first name Martin?"

"Naw—I think it was more sophisticated, like Walter, Harold, or something…but he's probably had a lot of aliases. He's rather dark—probably from the Mideast."

"Does this look anything like him?" asked Kavinsky who suddenly stopped flipping the pages on booked suspects. "Yeah—that could be the slime ball," McKay nodded.

"And if you put a beard on him and sideburns he'd probably come up looking like this…right?" Kavinsky updated the picture in the file with some scribbling under the nose.

"You're a lousy artist…have you seen someone like this?" probed McKay.

"Yep. He may be working at one of our local executive exercise clubs with the handle of Martin not Walter," responded Joe.

"Let me know if I can be of help….I'd love to work him over. For some reason, he's always been a slippery ass and ends up out of the joint as fast he's put in," scowled the narc officer.

Kavinsky thought he'd pay another call on the pool But he was reminded by one of the deputies that he first had to visit with Mrs. Sims about the reported breakin at her house. Before he could put his jacket on again, however, his cell phone rang. It was Sarah Crimmons.

"Hi"—she said softly for openers. "Let's do dinner tonight."

"Hi," he replied. "Sounds great…your place or mine?" the cop shot back.

"I know it's late to ask, Joe, but Susan's having a friend over and she hoped we could join them at our place and perhaps go out for a few drinks afterwards," she explained. Realizing Sarah was still in need of a shoulder to lean on after her mother's tragedy, he gently responded, "Let's do it. I'll see you at 7…okay?"

"It's a date! See you then. And Joe…thanks! I'm having a rough time coping."

Glancing at his watch to make sure he wasn't late for his mid-morning appointment with Mrs. Sims, Joe flung his coat over his shoulder and gulped down the last of his cooling coffee. But before he got two feet from his desk his phone rang again. This time it was his uncle Al.

"Hey Joey...glad I caught you. How about lunch at Toby's this noon? I got some new input which could help you on that Sims case."

"It'll have to be a late one, unc. Matter of fact, I've got to see Mrs. Sims in a few minutes about that breakin at her place." He could sense some urgency in his uncle's voice. "Look, unc. I'll try to cut it short out there. I'm sure I can see you around noon-neesh—about12:30."

He then headed out the door to his unmarked car and drove toward the impressive Sims estate in the exclusive River Heights suburb just north of St. Paul, where many of the community's top professional people reside in mansions bordered by iron fences and secured by guard stations.

Amid such grandeur, Kavinsky almost felt that he would be greeted by a butler when he used the knocker on the large door. Instead, an attractive middle-aged woman answered. She looked rather weary, and he assumed this must be Sims'widow.

He was invited into a spacious and elegant living room which was rather messed up, apparently by the person or persons who broke in while she was still at her husband's service. A few moments of chatting with Mrs. Sims led the lieutenant to the real purpose of his visit, namely: what were the intruders looking for?

"I don't really know, Mr. Kavinsky. They certainly didn't take anything I could notice. They simply ramsacked everything imaginable as though they were searching for something special and couldn't find it." She added, "With Frank's drowning and all, I just can't imagine why anyone would want to do something like this."

Joe tried again to get to the point. "Mrs. Sims...", but he was suddenly interrupted with "please call me Adel." He cleared his throat mostly out of surprise by this informality in such a formal setting. and continued, "Adel, do you know anything about a key the judge was wearing?" Noticing her quizzical look, he explained "this may have some bearing on the tragedy."

"Believe me, Mr. Kavinsky, this is the very first time I've heard about a key. I had no idea that anything like a special key belonged to Frank. His pool locker had a combination lock as far as I know."

"Did he have diabetes?...or take injections for any reason?" the detective inquired further.

"Certainly not...he was in fine health," declared the widow. "Why do you ask? Is there something I should know about?"

At this point, he looked straight into the eyes of the widow, to see what reaction he might have obtained so far, and, most of all, to note any indication whatsoever of her skirting the truth. From his police training, he found that most liars do not look you in the eye directly and that they flush just a bit around the cheeks. But he could see no reaction of any kind. Instead, she looked right back at him directly, apparently intent on knowing more about what he was trying to say.

"I'm not sure, yet," he responded. "Did you and your husband communicate much about his work at all?"

She seemed to ponder over this question before replying. "Perhaps not in the way we should have." Turning to look at a picture on a lamp-table of what appeared to be a family gathering, she continued, "The judge and I very seldom talked about anything but family matters—schooling for the kids, upcoming vacation...that sort of thing. Really, he never brought his business up, and I got the message that he didn't want me to pry into it."

"I realized he traveled in a special circle and that they had their confidentialities.

I often wondered what was going one, though. I always hoped—and prayed—that nothing was wrong."

Joe nervously cleared his throat, but couldn't help but feel more at ease. He sensed she may be leveling with him, but for some reason he still thought she may be holding back something.

"Adele, I want you to promise me that you'll tell no one about my visit or about our discussion." He paused, then added, "and please…trust me. I'm just trying to put pieces together. The key…the diabetes…this all may be nonsense. It's much too soon to sort fiction from fact."

With this, he looked at his watch and arose from his chair. "I'll keep you well informed. If you want to get in touch with me here's my card. By all means, let me know if there are any further breakins or problems of any kind."

As he approached the door, he asked—as if the thought just came to him—"oh by the way, did the judge have any tattoos on him?"

The widow's smile vanished. "None that I know of, why?"

"No wonder. The coroner said they were too tiny to spot. With cremation they're gone forever anyhow—right?" Joe shrugged, looking at her with his most serious expression. "Just remember Adele—be sure to keep me posted."

"Thank you lieutenant. I'll keep that in mind. You can be assured I'll tell no one about our conversation."

As Kavinsky drove once again around the picturesque hills of River Heights to meet his uncle Al downtown, he wondered how many of the affluent in this winding beautiful community really made their money on the straight and narrow. He couldn't help but think that judge Sims must have had something on the sideburners besides his law practice to afford such classy living. And he still wasn't sure if Adel Sims was really being completely truthful with him.

Sure enough, Al was waiting for his nephew at Toby's when he arrived. Traditionally, Benjamin was always the first person at the scene. It must have something to do with his nose for news, thought Joe.

"Hi unc, hope I haven't kept you waiting long." He noted that Al had been once again scribbling on his napkin. "I give up…what do all these marks say?"

"They say you've got to watch yourself, Joe," replied Al with a grin. "Something smells fishy…and I don't mean from the kitchen here." The detective was aware that his uncle was concerned for his welfare, maybe too much at times.

"Okay, what do you have for me now news hawk?", knowing full well that Al had been digging some more into the Sims case.

"I'm not sure, kid, but we may be in deeper than we think. I found out that Sims may be connected to a drug network that goes right back to where they grow the stuff."

Upon downing some more beer, Al added, "Also that so-called swim club of yours may be filled with his narc friends. Sloan is just a lightweight in all of this. There's some real kingpins involved, Joe, and you don't know who's really on first."

Kavinsky listened intently as he munched on the free popcorn on the table. This time keeping his eyes on his uncle.

"Any suspects besides Sloan?"

"Only hunches, Joey, only hunches" shrugged Al. "But I have this gut feeling that anyone interfering doesn't last too long."

After another swig of beer, Benjamin added thoughtfully, "For one thing, I have a theory about what happened to Sims at that pool."

"Yeah, tell me about it," his nephew encouraged as he caught a glimpse of a swinging hip passing by belonging to a redhead on the arms of a guy old enough to be her daddy. She winked at Joe as she strolled toward the bar.

Looking down at his scribbled napkin, Al remarked, "Well I think there may have been two people with separate missions in the pool with the judge. One, part of the judge's group waiting to get something from him like an important paper or to give him something, and the other—someone in on the plan—who instead gave the judge the needle."

Joe didn't respond. He just sat there looking at his uncle quizzically. "Man what have you been drinking?" he finally asked. "Why wouldn't they just give one another whatever they wanted at a private meeting rather than in the water?"

"I told you it was just a hunch. But I would guess they didn't want to create any unnecessary suspicions. That whoever was closing in was so close it was safer to get together as they always do—at their regular times at lap swim."

Joe lit a cigarette, then blew the smoke up in the air smiling. He didn't wisecrack this time, however. "And who do you think did this dirty deed?"

"I have no idea, Joe. I guess it was tough to tell one swimmer from the next with their goggles on. Also, I understand they've allowed women to lap swim now with the men at that club."

The cop took another drag on his cigarette, thinking what his uncle was saying. "Yeah, I know. It may have been someone that Sims didn't know anything about, a woman swimmer for that matter. Someone least expected, but apparently a whiz with a needle."

With that, Joe thought out loud, "Could have been a doctor or someone very familiar with the human anatomy." Cripes, with the terrorist war going on there might even be some tie-in with parts of the Mideast where heroin is trafficked." But after giving this more thought, he added "however the female body is mostly hidden in those areas isn't it."

"Well, I'm sure you know a lot about the women anatomy," kidded his uncle as he wiped his mouth and gazed at the clock. "Gotta Go, Joe, I found out at the last moment that I have to read the first run-edition this afternoon."

"Hey—don't forget to tear up that napkin, unc. No evidence, please. As you know, the whole world may be in on this as it is," the policeman chuckled.

Following his uncle's departure, the lieutenant looked for a phone. He remembered he wanted to find out if Sloan was going to be around at the club that day. A quick call to the club's front desk informed him that the janitor was gone for the day.

That was okay. Kavinsky needed time to check the books at the club to find out who belonged and who were some of the women sharing the pool at the time Sims was swimming.

When he arrived at the club he immediately ran into Lillian at the front desk. Her attiitude was about as cold as the water in the pool. To get her attention he flashed his police badge. With this, Lillian then quickly informed him that the club does not keep records on daily swimmers for more than a few hours.

"There's no copies or anything, even on a weekly basis?" he questioned.

"I'm afraid that's the way it is. We have so many people in and out that our place would be cluttered with paperwork," explained the apparently too-busy receptionist.

"But surely there's a swimming club roster? These guys have been swimming together for years I understand."

"I have no records. Perhaps you should check with some of the early morning swimming club participants."

"Anyone in particular?"

"Perhaps our manager, Mr. Lawrence, would know. He'll be in later this afternoon. I suggest you call for an appointment, however," said the tight-lipped receptionist.

The lieutenant shrugged, looked at his watch, and determined that he was wasting time. After asking Lillian to have the manager call him and giving her his card, he proceeded toward the exit. Before reaching the door, however, he bumped into an old buddy, Joel Swanson, who joined the Army with him right after high school.

Swanson, now a day trader in stocks, gave Kavinsky the name of someone who he believed was once in the swim group but may have left since moving away from the community.

The name, Stan Sherman, didn't ring a bell with the cop. At least he was no VIP as far as Joe knew, and obtaining a name or two from Sherman shouldn't pose any threat to him from other club members.

Once back at his precinct, Kavinsky ran a check on Sherman. He was pretty clean…a business grad, cashier, and former insurance sales rep. The cop surmised that perhaps Sherman was invited to join the club because of his financial connections with some of the more powerfully influential members.

With that in mind, Joe tried calling Sherman's home to obtain his business number. Surprisingly, he reached Sherman himself. After some brief introductions, kavinsky felt the person on the other end of the line sincerely wanted to be helpful.

Seems Sherman had read about Sims' reported drowning, but wasn't present at the pool when this happened since he left the group a few months before being laid off at a downtown St. Paul savings and loan office when the S&Ls took a dive and many went belly up. Sherman, like so many others caught in the S&L downturn, turned to day-trading and consulting from his office at home. He admitted that his new lifestyle is rather lonely and that he may consider joining the club again just to have some good opportunities to socialize with others.

Sherman wasn't sure about the current membership, but he did recall there were a few female newcomers. Apparently comfortable that Kavinsky's inquiries were just routine police business following the Sims incident, Sherman tried to remember if he heard the names of any of the new members, either men or women.

"There were some after I left," remarked Sherman, who added jokingly, "Maybe they were just waiting for me to leave. I'm not much of a swimmer you know." He paused, then thoughtfully continued, "just a minute, I do recall there was a doctor that joined. But what was her name?" As if to answer his own question, he snapped his fingers and said: "Yeah—I believe it was Nancy….Nancy Stein, no…Nancy, uh…Nancy Klein? That's it, Dr. Nancy Klein. There was another gal, too, works in a store. I believe her name sounds like Suzanna…starts with the letter S."

Kavinsky asked, "Do you know anything more about Nancy…where she practices, how long she's been going to the club?"

"Not really. I heard she's a specialist of sorts, but don't know where."

"Is she a pretty good swimmer?" probed the detective.

"I don't know that either. But anyone able to join the advanced swimming group has to be able to keep up with the others—to go like a fish without coming up for air," laughed Sherman.

"Yeah, I'm sure of that," responded Kavinsky as he recalled the tough time he had lap swimming recently at the pool. His arm muscles were still sore from that workout.

"You've been most helpful, Mr. Sherman. Since we're still investigating, I would appreciate it if you did not mention our conversation to anyone at this time," requested the cop.

Checking his watch upon hanging up, Kavinsky went again to his files and a department computer to see if he had any input on either of the two women swimmers. There were lots of women with names starting with the letter s…but no Suzanna's. Strangely enough, however, there was a slight police record after the doctor's name.

The files showed that back about seven years ago Nancy Klein, before becoming an MD, was caught sniffing cocaine at a party thrown by a group of heroin addicts in an apartment near the university. Must have been while she was in med school, he figured.

Joe once again referred to his narc pal McKay. "Got anything on a Dr. Nancy Klein, Mac?…she apparently was a coke sniffer, but she's probably straight now and one whiz of a swimmer."

"Another one of your fitness freaks out of control at that crazy gym?" asked McKay sarcastically. "You know the more I think about it, that so-called fitness center could very well be a center for drug dealers."

McKay shrugged, "Nope, that name doesn't ring a bell, pal. But you might want to check the U's records—sometimes they keep copies of reports on their students and grads."

Kavinsky began making some calls. The first paid off, thanks to McKay. Yes, the school did keep resumes and yes, they did have some still on file on Dr. Klein. They would not, however, read the report back since anyone interested would have to personally call on their personnel office for permission and access to such information.

Keeping in mind he had to be at a party with Sarah that evening, the lieutenant drove somewhat faster than usual as he made his way to the university. When he finally got to the right desk, showing off his police badge quickly opened the right files to him.

He wasn't quite sure what to look for, but he did find out that Klein was indeed a star swimmer. In fact, she won medals in nearly all events at the U and following that tried out for the Olympics for six months or so. She had a very impressive resume, indeed. Everything was positive. A brilliant student, rich parents our East, and a top scholar in her medical class.

"Wow," said Kavinsky, almost to the distraction of others around him in the quiet study hall. "What a lady! she does everything well"—maybe even with a needle, he thought, although it was difficult to figure why she would ever go bad with all the good things she had going. "She's a perfect 10—and with all that she's probably a terrific looker," Joe whispered to himself.

Upon jotting down a few notes, he headed out the library door realizing he should be freshening up for his big date with Sarah. On his way to his apartment, he fondled the notes tucked inside his coat pocket while still thinking what a babe this Nancy must be.

By the time he arrived at the Crimmon's Joe was all set for romance—complete with a dousing of his favorite cologne which, he hoped, would once again turn Sarah on to his advances.

She met him at the door, in a very tight fitting dress that gave him the urge to make love to her right there in the doorway. And he might have done just that, except for the fact that he couldn't help but notice in the background some tall stranger who was standing next to her sister observing his grand entrance.

"Joe, honey, I'd like you to meet Frank Meyers," greeted Sarah, turning to the grinning couple behind her. "Frank and Susan would like to join us tonight. They're just like two peas in a pod, you might say," Sarah giggled glancing at her sister in her cute little girl fashion.

"Hi ya Joe…Susan tells me you're a cop. Don't worry, I'll make her be on her very best behavior tonight," chortled Susan's oversized muscular, wavy-haired boy friend. Joe sized him up as a control freak as he watched Frank grab Susan and, much to her surprise, kiss her passionately for about several minutes.

CHAPTER 9

Frank turned out to be a real obstacle in the path of romance for Joe throughout the night, not to say a genuine pain in the ass. It seemed every time that Joe had a chance to whisper sweet nothings to Sarah, Meyers butted in with some stupid remark When they finally got to an intimate drinking spot after dinner in a downtown hotel, Joe immediately took Sarah to the small dance floor even through the music was hard rock. An awkward dancer at best, he was soon ready to give up, especially when the musicians went wild.

When they returned to their table, Frank was waiting, all smiles and ready to continue with more dull conversation—almost to the embarrassment of Susan, thought Joe. At this point, the sisters decided to visit the ladies room. This left Joe and Frank looking at one another. Joe broke the silence by suggesting that they doff their jackets in this hot and swinging environment.

Since he left his gun and holster in the locked glove compartment of his car, as was his custom when out to forget the office, he wasn't concerned about revealing his shirt sleeves. Meyers did likewise. When Joe took out a cigarette, his burly companion suggested that he try his new lighter instead and extended a tattooed arm to show off the expensive looking lighter.

However, as Meyer's was ready to flick the wick of his new lighter, Joe noticed something other than a tattoo when Frank's rolled-up sleeve slid nearly back to his elbow. The cop wasn't exactly sure what he saw and pretended not to get a good light. To make sure, he asked for another try.

Meyers reached over again and flicked the lighter. This time, Joe spotted what he was looking for—some needle scratches on Frank's forearm and what looked like a couple of "narc marks."

The detective's first thought was that this creep's an addict. He tried to quickly look away and hoped Frank didn't' catch him eyeing the marks. This was neither the time nor place to discuss this with Susan's large, obnoxious escort. But he couldn't help but wonder why she wanted to be seen with such a jerk.

Looking out at the dance floor, he heard Meyers ask him how he liked his job as a cop. Trying to be friendly while the girls were still primping, Joe went through his typical response for school kids and old ladies. "It's like any other job, Frank, sometimes there's action, sometimes there's not. But you always have to be ready," he shrugged. But Frank wasn't going to let it rest at that

And asked, "I'll bet you get some pretty interesting cases."

"Yeah, once in awhile. But mostly it's just routine stuff."

"I know what ya mean. Me, I'm in real estate. Sometimes you can't make a dime, other times you're raking it in."

Sipping some more gin and tonic, Frank continued, "Susan tells me you're checking into the Judge Sims drowning. God, what a tragedy that was. That guy had everything. The firm I'm with may be involved in selling his home. His widow wants something smaller, I understand." There was silence again as Joe looked at Meyers. The stare-down didn't last long since Frank then asked, "You making any progress? I understand everyone seems to be wondering how the hell this could have happened to the judge. The widow doesn't want to stay around their home. She said there's just too many memories."

This was news to Joe. The judge's wife certainly didn't indicate she was moving when he visited her. And how did this guy know anything about the Sims investigation?…he only mentioned this to a select and trusty few. He knew uncle Al wouldn't tell his own wife if he was even working on a PTA story. He recalled, however, that in addition to McKay in Narc and via his confidential work report to the police chief, he also casually made some inquiries with the lifeguard, the crabby bitch at the club, and his old reliable friend who knew Sherman.

Before he could figure out a reply, the ladies returned from the rest room. Joe hoped Sarah had time to tell her sister what an air-head she was dating. He lost no time in getting Sarah back again on the dance floor to break away from him.

Fortunately, the music was slow and soft this time around. He could finally get close to his lover and keep Meyers from his mind. However, he couldn't help but notice when swinging Sarah around that Frank seemed more interested in gazing at him and Sarah then talking to Susan. In fact, he thought, Meyers seemed very pre-occupied at making sure he was keeping Joe and Sarah in his sights as much as possible.

Despite the fact that Meyers made for an awfully long night, Joe was up immediately when his alarm went off bright and early the next morning. After finishing off some bad coffee, he got Sarah on the phone to let her know his early schedule and sort of apologize as to why he had to bug out early from Frank's "party." But his loud beeper went off and nearly upset the conversation.

"You still wearing that horrible beeping machine?" she asked. "Yep, I gotta get up for a swim and needed a reminder," Joe explained.

"You're kidding," said Sarah. "Nope," responded Joe nonchalantly, "I'm a member of the early morning swim club at Executive Workout." As Sarah pondered this, he took advantage of her early morning grogginess by inquiring further about Frank and his relationship with Susan.

"Oh, Frank…he's just an acquaintance. A guy she met at the Sims funeral. He was with Sapel, a good friend of daddy's."

"Did she go to bed with him?" Joe asked. "Are you kidding?" replied Sarah. "No-never. At least I don't think so. I heard Frank drive away shortly after you left." She frowned, "Why—what's the matter don't you like Frankie baby?" Joe shrugged, "No—he's a big creep."

Sarah teased, "He's that bad, huh? How sad—he's so cute."

"As my mother says: 'pretty is as pretty does,'"Joe said with a shrug.

With that, Sarah suddenly became suddenly serious "Well my mother told me a lot, too. For one thing, she told me how terrible people can be if they don't like you and want you out of the way. Before she and daddy split, she used to tell me how certain wealthy people in this town could push others around to get what they want."

"Was it drugs they wanted?" the cop interrupted.

"Joe, yes…it's out of control. Mom said he told her that bankers, judges and lots more are all part of our local drug scene…even in and outside the state and overseas."

"Why are you telling me this now?"

"Because I don't want you hurt. I was always too afraid to repeat what mom was saying. She said they could hurt Susan and me. They're vicious and even hire hit men. Mom said she met one in a banker's office while waiting for daddy one day. He was arguing with the bank president about something and dad said he was getting a contract on someone."

"Yeah—I may have met one last night," Joe noted, "and your mom may have met one in the garage." Sarah responded, "I know…I guess I'm taking her death harder than Susan. Even though we're twins she's always been the strongest." Sarah suddenly snapped her fingers when mentioning her sister and said, "I almost forgot, Susan and I are going to work this morning. I better wake her up!"

CHAPTER 10

When Sarah and Susan Crimmons stroll down the street you look twice. In many ways, it's like seeing double, especially when they decide to dress alike, even though they usually do their shopping at different stores.

Even Joe sometimes had a difficult time telling them apart. Sarah was gentler, softer, Joe felt; whereas Susan had a more aggressive, tougher side. Nearly everyone knew them around northeast—called "Nordeast" by the natives—Minneapolis where they grew up. They didn't have to say a thing—just saunter down the street in their pretty little hip-swinging fashion. Very often, however, they weren't on the way to shopping but enroute to working. Sarah was employed at Nieman Marcus on fifth and Susan at Sak's on sixth.

It was during one of their occasional work breaks together on a sunny day that they ran into Ernie Morris, a friend of their dad's. Morris, a slick salesman with plenty of charm for the ladies, beamed his widest smile upon encountering the twins. Without being invited, he immediately sat down at their small table under a restaurant awning.

The sisters regarded Morris as somewhat sinister and always in search of information. But you never really knew what he was after. Their father said Ernie belonged to the Sapel mob. "A nice guy, but don't ever trust him," he warmed.

"Greetings girls!—or should I say women considering the protocol of the day?" With that opening, Morris indicated to the waiter that he wanted to order. The sisters had just sat down and were checking their purses for coffee money.

"Ah, ah…this is on me." He added, "What a day brightner to bump into Zack's beautiful daughters." Both Sarah and Susan knew it was almost too coincidental.

He immediately began prying. "What's old Zack up to these days? You know, I never see him around much anymore. I suppose you two travel around to be with him at times."

"We guess he's pretty busy, it's hard for us to keep up with him, too, Ernie," responded Sarah.

"I'm sure he is. I miss him. It was nice knowing he was nearby. I don't really see too many of the old gang anymore," said Morris as he reached for a cigar in a shirt pocket. The twins, knowing they were in for lots of second-hand smoke, squirmed as they thought how to escape from the boring guy.

"If you hear from your dad, or see him, let him know how much he's missed by his pals," said Morris, blowing a puff of smoke their way. "I remember when you were just little girls following him around. He was real proud of you. I'm sure you want to keep in touch with him, especially with your mom gone and all."

"You probably know more about him than we do, Ernie," remarked Susan. "What have you heard lately?"

This twist in conversation seemingly took some of the smoke out of Morris. Coughing briefly, he flicked his ashes and replied hesitantly, "Nothing at all…no one has heard anything from your old man including Sapel or any of his business contacts.

"You ladies are about his only close relatives aren't you?"

Sensing that Morris was getting too nosy, Sarah looked at her watch and rapidly downed some more coffee. "Yes, at least his closest. Look

Ernie we have to be getting back to work. Keep us posted if you hear anything and we'll do likewise, okay?"

Morris' smile faded as he took a card out of his other shirt pocket. "Yeah, sure…keep my calling card handy and give me a buzz if you find out anything. I sure would like to keep in touch with him. You know, absence makes the heart grow fonder, or something like that."

"Is there something special you want to talk to him about?" asked Sarah as she and Susan prepared to leave.

"Not exactly—just wanted to know what he's been up to—you know, to keep updated." Walking back to their jobs took only a few minutes by way of the Nicollet Mall. Susan had to continue walking several more blocks upon leaving Sarah who headed into the shopping complex housing Nieman Marcus. An elevator was near the center of the complex that went to all floors of the retail stores in the center. Two other elevators nearby also stopped at all floors but were mostly for business people on way to the fourth and fifth floors where rental and real estate offices were located.

Sarah pushed the button for the second floor, but nothing happened. She noticed that the floor indicator above the elevator pointed to the third floor and was holding. Obviously someone was using it as a freight elevator again, she thought somewhat annoyed. Glancing at her watch once more, she realized she was close to being late.

At this point, one of the business elevators opened and Sarah rushed to get on before the doors closed. Upon entering, she sensed that there was another person in the elevator, who obviously got on in the basement. It was a man. He had his coat collar up and was almost hidden in the far corner of the elevator.

Turning around she noticed a middle-aged guy grinning at her. She pretended to be oblivious to him and only intent on getting to Nieman Marcus on the third floor. But all the while, she could feel his stare going up and down her body. Sarah nervously kept looking at the arrow above the door indicating the progress of the elevator, as though trying to push it up faster. Between second and third, however, the elevator suddenly jerked, stalled and then completely stopped.

For a moment, it seemed like the whole world stopped with it. Everything became deathly silent in the elevator. Even the air-conditioning quit and the lights dimmed.

Suffering from mild claustrophobia, Sarah was terror stricken at first. Not knowing what to do, she looked back at her companion in the faulty elevator for some reassurance. He simply kept staring at her with that same silly grin.

Finally, the stranger spoke up. "I can make it go again, lady. But I need some help from you."

What kind of help?" asked Sarah frightened upon hearing his low, sinister voice.

"Where's your old man?" he inquired.

"What do you mean? Who wants to know?" replied the alarmed young woman boldly.

"The mob does. He has some information we want. You tell me, and up goes the elevator. No one gets hurt. I know all about elevators—how they go, how to get out."

As he came closer to Sarah, she frantically began pushing the button warning that the elevator was stuck. She could already feel his hot breath but thought she heard some noise above hopefully indicating that perhaps rescuers were already on the way to help. She pushed the alarm again.

'What the hell you doing sister, get your finger off that button!" commanded her attacker. He reached inside his coat for a gun and held it firmly to her head.

But Sarah pushed even harder causing the loud alarm to be heard throughout many levels of the building. Despite its steady sound, she also began to hear more clearly the words from the workers trying to get the elevator moving again.

The burly hood grabbed her hair and slapped her across the face as he wrenched her finger from the alarm. At that point, some of the workers could be heard yelling: "Don't panick, we almost have it fixed."

With that, the tall, thin stranger let go of Sarah, now bleeding from her lip, and jumped up and down in the elevator until his hand was able to grasp and push one of the top panels loose from the elevator ceiling. As though he was an acrobat, he wiggled himself up through the hole where the panel was and disappeared. But Sarah could still hear him above her as he apparently began trying to climb one of the cables to a floor where he could escape.

She could hear him yell, "I'll be back to get you. Count on it. You and your old man and sister are dead meat." The fleeing man made his fast getaway before the rescuers could get to the frightened young woman in distress. She began crying, wiping the blood from her face, and thanked God that Susan was in a building without elevators.

Sarah was still trembling from fright when the doors of the elevator were finally pulled back to release her.

After telling her story to her rescuers and the mall's security personnel, she phoned Joe to let him know what happened. The lieutenant calmly reasoned that perhaps Sapel wanted her father for either a bad debt or a bad promise.

He joined Sarah for lunch in the mall, attempting to comfort her. She was almost too upset to talk about what occurred in the elevator, assuring him only that she was not raped or otherwise attacked. But her face and neck still hurt somewhat.

The lieutenant figured that Ernie's questioning and the elevator guy's threats tied in too much. He theorized that both were commissioned by the Sapel gang to find out how to get to Zack through his daughters. Judging from what she and her sister said, they couldn't get any answers.

"The police may track that elevator thug down. He must have left some prints to get out of the place," said Joe "As for Morris, we'll keep an eye on him. We can't press any charges until he gets bolder."

"You think he may?" asked his nervous girlfriend. "Maybe," cautioned Joe. "It depends on hard Sapel pushes."

CHAPTER 11

Besides looking out for his lover and keeping his uncle happy, Joe had all he could do to make sure his job wasn't in jeopardy. The police chief seemed more demanding than ever that he spend most of his time trying to catch embezzlers on the north side of Minneapolis than he did regarding the Sims matter. Joe had to sneak in some time to find out what Sloan knew. But despite all this, he gave first priority to Sloan the morning after the elevator incident.

Sloan wasn't around, however, when he got to the club. Lillian was at her station and let him know quite coldly that the head janitor did not report in. Scratching his head, Joe asked if manager Lawrence was available. He was told the manager was on vacation.

"I asked you the other day to have Lawrence call me," scolded Joe. "This is a police matter lady. Where can I reach Sloan?"

She stopped her paper work at the stern tone of his voice and looked up. "I have no idea…he has an unlisted phone number."

"I want his address—where does he live?" he demanded.

"I believe it's on Yale street officer," she said rather meekly when she saw the cop's badge. "It's in St.Paul."

"Yale and what?" pursued the cop. "Yale and Brower…in an old red brick apartment."

"What's the address and apartment number?"

"I'm not sure. He didn't tell me. The apartment's on the corner. I think his name's on the lobby directory."

"You think so, huh? Tell Lawrence I'm waiting to hear from him!"

Before leaving, he remembered to ask Lillian one more thing. "Oh, by the way, did the judge have a shower room locker and a locker key?"

Apparently surprised by the question, Lillian hesitated before replying, "No, I understand he was always in a hurry and dressed near the shower room. Besides, our lockers all have combination locks, no need for keys."

Joe spent his drive-time to the apartment building trying to figure out what kind of key was around the judge's neck. Upon his arrival, the detective, armed with a revolver but no search warrant, found the door of the apartment building unlocked and the directory posted in the hall. The place smelled like an unkempt footlocker. Sloan's name and room number were scribbled in pencil on the directory like an after-thought.

Kavinsky felt lucky that at least the apartment was on the first floor since he didn't want to be in this dump for long. As usual, he knocked on the door and stepped to one side, remembering his police training in case the occupant wasn't too friendly.

He knocked several times but no one answered. He tried the doorknob and was surprised that the door was unlocked and so in need of repair that it opened slightly with just a turn of the knob. Kavinsky felt his gun under his coat for more confidence and then walked in carefully. The main room still had the lights on and appeared to be well furnished, probably with the same stuff Sloan moved around with him as he escaped the law. After shouting out "police"—Joe looked around. There was only one bedroom and the bed was unmade as though someone recently left it or was waiting to get into it. He then checked the nearby kitchen where he spotted a few cans of beer on the table and food was still on a plate. He touched the cans noting that they were still slightly cold.

It was at this point that he heard a dripping sound, like the dripping of water from a faucet or shower. He looked for the bathroom, proceeding down a dimly lit hallway. Noticing a small light at the end of the hall, Joe reasoned that it probably was escaping from a room—most likely the bathroom—with its door left slightly ajar.

When he approached the door, the dripping became louder and he spotted water seeping from under the door. He took a deep breath, as though preparing for the worst, and then kicked the door wide open with his foot and hurtled himself into the room ready to struggle with Sloan. But this all proved to be a waste of effort.

Kavinsky almost knew what to expect. He finally found his man—a guy he simply wanted to question. Sloan was lying naked slumped in the bathtub with the water still running over on the tile floor. His eyes were open wide as if in surprise. The tub water was completely pink from his slashed wrists. Apparently, Sloan preferred suicide rather than answering questions and being put in the joint again, Kavinsky thought at first. But he wasn't too convinced. He noticed Sloan had an alarmed expression on his face, as if caught off guard by someone before the cop even made his entrance.

Joe also noted a few abrasions on the victim, other than the bruises and wrist cuts. In most cases, the police would shrug and write the death off as simply doing oneself in, but there were too many suicides turning up in connection with the judge Sims case—with too many questions left unanswered, Joe felt. If he had time, he was sure he might also notice a needle mark on the body.

To avoid leaving his fingerprints, the cop wrapped his hand with a handkerchief and grasped the faucet handle, turning off the water. He noted that only the cold water tap was on. In fact, the bloody water was much too cold for anyone taking a bath. And it was unlikely that Sloan was bathing a long time since his beer was still cold, the lights lit, and food left on the table. He figured there should be at least a trace of warm water, perhaps near the bottom of the tub, but there wasn't. Why would anyone want a cold bath? If it was murder, he deduced, the murderer would probably turn on any tap available to make a fast getaway especially if he heard Joe coming.

Kavinsky, using his handkerchief again to avoid leaving prints, dialed police homicide. The chief would be as mad as hell because he had no search warrant. When two patrol cars from the nearby precinct arrived, along with an ambulance from the medical examiner's department,the lieutenant briefed the police officer in charge and prepared to take off to write up his report of the incident. He knew there would be questions about his whereabouts and the death. But before he got to the door another officer interrupted to point out that the police chief already wanted to hear from him before he left.

The phone in Sloan's apartment was being used, so Kavinsky used the public phone in the lobby on his way out. Chief Neil Cermak sounded upset. He greeted Joe by asking him why the hell he was spending so damn much time on a case like this when there were so many "more important" cases he should be covering. Cermak reminded him that if he had any spare time he should be focusing on solving the bank embezzlement problems occurring on the north side.

Kavinsky knew when he was being chewed out so he didn't interrupt until the chief was finished. He then quickly mentioned that he would be back at his desk in about an hour and would write a full report on this case that he felt was much bigger in scope than originally expected. After a pause at the other end of the line, the chief reminded the lieutenant that he'd make much faster progress back to his desk by avoiding highway 84 being torn up by construction and which Kavinsky would normally take. Cermak suggested going by way of the "short-line", which skirted the city by way of a rough and curvy road which ran next to some railroad tracks but which could knock at least 15 minutes off his driving time.

With that, Joe got in his car, put his gun back into the glove compartment, and took off for the short-cut the chief recommended. As he wheeled onto the line of traffic, he failed to spot a mid-sized sedan parked near Sloan's place starting up about a half-block behind him. In fact, he was well on his way on the short-line before noticing he had company on this rather isolated stretch of road leading to downtown.

Since there were no stop lights along the way, only a few yield intersections, the cop purposely accelerated his sporty vehicle, mostly to see if the driver behind was indeed intent on pursuing him. He was, and although the other car was a conservative-looking vehicle with muddy plates which helped to hide the license numbers, it apparently was souped up to keep pace. Recalling his FBI training a few years ago on following and ditching suspects, Joe kept his eyes peeled far ahead while glancing at the guys closing in from behind. He knew that if he could see enough shoulder on the side of this bumpy road he could brake fast and do a spin—hopefully enough to get him going quickly in the other direction. He wasn't sure, however, if the other driver wasn't second-guessing him and how well those bozos behind were armed.

At the thought of being armed, Joe recalled his .38 in the glove compartment. If he could stretch far enough from the steering wheel he could grab it. But this would be very tricky and dangerous since he was already going about 100 miles-per-hour. No other vehicle except his pursuer was in sight. About the only thing he could see other than the road he was churning up was a gravel pit a few miles ahead. If he could turn a little onto the gravel, there might be a chance he could do his spin. At least when he was braking, he could perhaps lean over and hopefully seize his gun and shoot it out with these thugs.

He let up on the gas just a bit when the gravel came closer, although the driver in back was almost on his tail at this time. Joe knew that if he slammed on the brakes at top speed he would end up in fragments all over the road. Since he didn't want the other driver to know he was easing up, his foot had to be extra gentle on the gas pedal. Joe also had to judge when the driver would only be a distance of a couple of cars away so he wouldn't be in his trunk when he slammed on the brakes.

"Now—do it!" Joe hollered to himself as he turned his wheels suddenly to the right and stamped hard on the brake. His car contacted some of the loose gravel and rocks from the gravel pile and with its wheels cocked did a screeching spin counter clockwise as the other car kept speeding ahead and away from him. Joe's hand, which was not on the steering wheel, all but clawed at the glove compartment for his gun as he fell to the leaning side of the car. His fingers found the compartment button and the door opened. While his one hand turned the wheel sharply, he seized the gun with the other as his car kept turning and spinning.

His calculations were right. Almost on the verge of turning over, his car ended facing in the other direction. He let up on the gas, but could see from his rear view mirror that the other driver had gone a long ways before being able to skid to a stop and was doing an about-face to head back toward his car. There was only one thing Joe figured he could do. He flung himself against the car door, which he never locked thanks to a police driving course cautioning him about being pinned inside locked cars, grabbed the handle, and then slid on his belly until falling out the door onto the rough surface of the concrete road.

It was no surprise to hear shots coming from the car bearing down on him. As he sprawled motionless on the gravel next to the road he pushed his face into it to avoid any head shots. He knew his attackers were firing away at the passenger side of his Ferrari, which he had been using that morning since it was impossible to obtain a regular patrol car. He also knew that at the speed they were going they would have to be more than several blocks away before they could completely stop and examine their dirty work. But he wasn't about to let them finish him off so easily.

With gun in hand, he raised his torso far enough off the road to get a good fix on the two guys he could see getting out of their vehicle. He didn't want them to get too close and a few shots from afar might scare them off. Any closer and they could get him readily in their sights.

Crouched behind his open car door, Joe took aim and squeezed the trigger, just about twirling the driver around with a bullet near his ear. Both hoods seemed startled, as Joe hoped they'd be. The two of them started shooting back, not really knowing where Joe was. To further confuse them, the cop, still crouched, ran to the rear of the car and continued firing as he peeked around the passenger side of the vehicle.

Kavinsky then ran to the driver's side, reached in and hollered for help to his precinct over the cell phone. All he could say when he got a response was that he was pinned down on the short-line. It was like an eternity before Joe saw a car with flashing lights racing down the road. The other guys, still puzzled by their surprised predicament, must have seen the lights too.

After a few more aimless shots, the hoodlums took off in the direction they came from, apparently determined to be miles away from the siren of the oncoming squad car.

When his police comrades arrived, Joe was still sitting on the ground in bewilderment, reloading his gun. There was no trace of the fleeing high-powered attack car. He briefed the officers somewhat and told them he would put all this in the detailed report to the chief which he still planned to make out when, and if, he ever got back to his precinct.

"I'd say you're one damn lucky, fellow," commented one of the officers. "This side of your car door is riddled by bullets. They must have been using a Uzy or something like that." The lieutenant looked sorrowfully at the plight of his beloved sports car, thinking of all the payments yet to be made and how it attracted his women friends.

"It'll still go," he said starting the engine. "But my insurance agent will wonder what the hell's going on I'm sure." Saying "thanks fellas…see ya around but next time drive faster," Joe limped his car back to the precinct and called his insurance agent and a garage for the bad news about repairs. In fact, he became so immersed in thinking about the damaged vehicle that he nearly forgot to begin his report.

Before finding paper for the report, however, he was summoned to the chief's office.

It wasn't very often that Kavinsky got to interface directly with the head man of the force. Cermak was just another cop on the beat before being recently appointed chief for some reason. Joe had a hard time figuring that out since Cermak's track record on the force wasn't all that great.

He just didn't like the guy. Joe always regarded him as a politician who catered only to the rich and powerful. You wouldn't dare offend any of his affluent friends for fear of the chief's retaliation. It was quite obvious the chief liked to act the big shot role and wasn't afraid to put you down, or out, often in front of fellow officers if this made him feel important.

"Sit down Kavinsky," were the first words out of the chief's mouth when Joe entered his office. "I understand you ran into some problems this morning." Joe noticed Cermak wasn't alone, which was unfortunate since Joe was all set to go into details about what took place earlier in the day and to explain why he thought he didn't need a search warrant to knock on Sloan's door.

"You know Dave Paulson?" asked the chief gesturing to a tall middle-aged man standing near the chief's desk. Despite Paulson's heavy beard Kavinsky could detect a slight mirk on his face instead of a smile. "Yes— I thought you did," Cermak said as Joe nodded his head. "Good, because from now on you and Dave are partners."

Joe looked at Paulson who shifted his eyes to the chief. He had heard about Paulson's work on the force in the past. His record stunk. He was in on so many unnecessary shootings that complaints about his trigger-happy finger ran out of the department's file drawers.

"You'll do your own bank embezzlement snooping, okay? But anything more with that so-called drug case you're checking out will be done with Paulson, is that clear? And I still don't think there's anything to that shooting incident on short-line—probably just some guys figuring they owed you one for putting a pal away."

Holding his hand up to ward off interruptions, Cermak continued: "But I don't want to take any chances. Two guys are better than one when there's shooting going on."

"Doesn't matter much when they're using high powered attack guns," interrupted Kavinsky. "Two or ten can be taken out with just a pull of the trigger."

Cermak ignored this remark, continuing: "We'll look into it. Just remember to include Dave in on your work with the Sims matter and fill him in on what you've been doing. If this embezzlement gets any more serious around here I may have to pull you off the case entirely Kavinsky and let Dave here finish up on what you've been doing."

"What's wrong with McKay?" questioned Joe, wondering why hi narc friend wasn't considered. "I'd rather keep it between you and Dave at this point…if there's anything to it at all," explained Cermak. "Besides, Mac is up to his ears with other work."

The chief looked at his watch and concluded, "That's it guys. I've got to get on with it.And don't forget Kavinsky I still want a full report on my desk today about what happened this morning."

"Welcome podner," greeted Paulson as he walked out the door with Joe. Not wanting to be bugged any further by this new associate, Kavinsky told him he had to file his report before he could bring him into this matter. With that, Joe made his way back to his desk as if to attack his word processor.

Before he could sit down to figure out what was going on, however, he spotted a phone message. Someone scribbled on a post-it note almost illegibly: "Call your uncle…says he got something on Doc DeSantro and his girl friend Dr. Nancy.

CHAPTER 12

Al Benjamin set his coffee cup down and looked at the clock above the city desk. He just finished another headline and was waiting for some more business briefs when the phone rang. He sensed it was his nephew calling. Nearly all morning in the back of his mind he was thinking about Joe and the information he turned up on Klein and DeSantro.

"Joey, I've been doing some checking. I'm sure DeSantro pulled a double-cross on Sapel," Al almost whispered over the phone as openers. "The wire service reports that his plane blew up around Bimini island…near a little spot where Robert Beck hangs out in his drug empire. Nancy Klein just happened to be in Nassau when doc took off from there and I'll bet they got together before then."

Joe didn't comment. Al could quickly tell that his nephew didn't feel much like chatting. On sensing his nephew's hesitancy, he told him he'd call back later when it was a better time to talk.

The reporter wanted to do some further research, anyway, and when he got a little break from the copy desk he contacted the Bimini air service in Nassau for more information about the plane DeSantro was on. He was told it was a six-place Beechcraft that originated from Nassau, with one stop at Bimini and then on to Miami. However, he was puzzled over where the hell the doctor was coming from when he boarded the flight to Bimini. He was suppose to be in Central

America with his parents according to the assistant ME. Doc Erickson, Al recalled. Would Erickson be able to explain this?

A quick call to the medical examiner's office surprisingly brought Erickson promptly to the phone. Apparently Loring had a day off, Al sighed. It was a big relief since Erickson's voice was much gentler to the ears than Loring's. He reminded Erickson that the last time they talked DeSantro was expected to be enroute to Central America—not visiting Nassau.

Erickson said DeSantro was definitely in Central America, he called him from Bogota, but he apparently took a different way home. Al asked more about DeSantro, about his family and his studies.

After some hesitation, Erickson said he didn't know much about the guy, but knew he was single and that he probably was born in Bogota since his parents are from there. "Are they still there?" Benjamin asked. Erickson said the parents live around a large rural estate in the town of Tolu, on the Caribbean coast about 450 miles north of Bogota where he was schooled prior to the U. of Minnesota.

"Is that anywhere near Colombia?" inquired Al. "Very near," replied the doctor.

This was much more than Benjamin had bargained for. Al thanked Erickson, who he knew would be chewed out royally by Loring if he overheard the conversation, and was all set to hang up when the doctor added that DeSantro left a note for the reporter

"He said for you to say hello to Pelot." Erickson, knowing a little French, could be heard chuckling over the rhyme of the little note. "I don't know what this means, but maybe you do. That Ramon…always a kidder. He was always trying to make things rhyme a little around here. He was a nice guy. We'll certainly miss him'

Al scratched his head. "Yeah—what the hell is a Pelot?" He got no response, but he was mostly thinking about one thing—Colombia— home of the drug cartels. Sure, DeSantro had flown there with the key he obtained off Sims, all the while leading everyone to believe he gave the mysterious numbers to Sims' wife to distract and ward off Sapel's goons. And this was why Sims' home was ramsacked. The doc probably came home with a bag full of money which they wanted.

Now all the reporter had to do was to put the missing pieces together. He knew that up to now all this was still just his imagination at work. While not at his daily newspaper tasks he had to find a way to get more information on Dr. Nancy, Sapel as well as some affluent citizens of the Twin Cities, and maybe even some important residents of the Bahamas. The first thing he wondered about was if Nancy was back home. If Sapel was out money, which DeSantro meant to drop off with the cartel at Bimini, Sapel would be very upset, unless...and Al's mind wandered again, he and Klein had this all planned. At this point Al's fingers also began wandering through the phone book and listings of the many type doctors in the physician section. It took some time before he realized maybe she was not a general practitioner and started checking neurologists. Neurology....diseases of the nervous system...this could relate to knowing how to paralyze the nervous center with an injection, and knowing the latest methods to do so by those like the terrorists, thought Al.

He lucked out. There she was—Dr. N.B. Klein, doctor of nervous disorders. No big advertisement...just a small ad under other doctor names. Her office was in the downtown Minneapolis physician's building. Thinking his plan over for a second or two, he began dialing her phone number for an appointment.

When the phone rang, Dr. Klein's receptionist answered. He immediately wanted to know if the doctor was in, and was advised that she was on her hospital rounds and would be back that afternoon. "She's been gone for awhile hasn't she?" probed Benjamin.

"Yes, but Dr. Klein is now back from vacation and will be available for office calls for the rest of this month," volunteered the receptionist. "What time do you wish to see her and what seems to be the problem?"

Al thought fast, "I'm having some numbness in my arms and understand this could be a result of an old injury. I have a lot of pain and sure hope she can see me soon."

"The doctor could see you tomorrow morning at 10," the receptionist said after a pause.

Al considered his schedule, noting that tomorrow looked pretty flexible. "Okay—let's make it then…I'm Al Benjamin, over on Tyrone Road."

Upon hanging up, Benjamin wondered if it was smart to have mentioned his right name. Chances are, however Dr. Klein would not bother to question her patients' authenticity too much, as long as there were some bucks connected to the visit. Anyway, he figured he had to take some risks if he were to pursue this matter any further.

He knew, too, that he should become better acquainted with his subject if he ever planned to do an expose on this apparent very weird cocaine mess. All he had to go on at this point were comments his nephew tossed out over lunch about Dr Klein. Perhaps he could better size her up during a patient-to-doctor relationship. At least he might obtain some further glimpse into the makeup of this lady doc to help determine if she really was the sinister type individual he and Joe envisioned.

He began to doodle on a sheet of copy paper, writing down points to remember while at the doctor's office. He didn't want to slip up in any way. First of all, he wondered if she appeared agile and strong enough to encounter a big guy like Sims much less be able to push a needle into him as she swam by so quickly. And secondly, he was very interested in knowing about how long she was in the Bahamas. He knew the day DeSantro's plane went down. If she stayed in the Bahamas much longer she may have made some contacts with someone else from the Twin Cities or elsewhere, perhaps splitting some of the money or using this person to conceal it for her—or for Sapel.

He also wondered how well Klein knew DeSantro. They may have attended the same medical class or something. For that matter, she

may have come off as his girl friend, betraying him as she may be
doing to others

But at this point it was all conjecture on his part. He may be wrong—
dead wrong. But death seemed to be entering into the pieces of this
puzzle much too often. Joey would have been the latest casualty, Al realized. "Goddam—this whole scenario is losing its subtlety and getting
too complex," he thought.out loud. What used to be apparent suicides
became direct gunshots. Regardless of what Joey said the local police
chief thought about this drug matter, the drama was now being aired
out in the open and was becoming much nastier. Some underworld
people seemed to be out to kill his nephew and Al had better try every
way he can to interfere with their plans since, after all, he was the guy
that brought his nephew into all this mess.

The more he thought about this, the more determined he got.
Instead of taking time out to have a leisurely lunch while scanning com-
petitor newspapers, Benjamin headed to the Executive Workout Club to
see if the manager could shed some light on what was bothering him.
Unlike Joe's bad luck in catching people at the club, Al snagged Harvey
Lawrence in his office just before Harvey was about to dash off to
another so-called meeting. He figured he got there before Lillian could
buzz the warning signal in Lawrence's office.

He pretended he was doing a followup feature story on the Sims'
death, since there were some very loose ends still to cover. Lawrence
seemed extremely fidgety, asking the reporter to come back when he
had more time. Benjamin, however, got in some quick questions
including, did the manager have any idea who was present in the pool
at the time? and were there any doctors on hand who could have
helped Sims?

Lawrence answered an abrupt no to all questions. This allowed Al to
point out that he heard that a Dr. Nancy Klein was present. The manager frowned, looking surprised. "What do you know about this Klein?"
Benjamin asked.

Lawrence's face, which showed he was upset by such questioning, turned a shade more red. "I don't know anything about her...only that she's a new member. I wasn't aware that she was at the pool at the time. There's no law against that I guess."

Al responded with a threatening look, "Hmm, this sure has the makings of an interesting story...no record of people present during swimming, possibly a doctor or two on hand—and yet absolutely no one around when the victim needed help."

"You're not going to print that?"

"I should," threatened Al. "there doesn't seem to be any information available, nor anything that suggests otherwise," noted Benjamin sensing he was on the way to drawing the frustrated manager out in the open so he'd break down and really tell what he knew.

"I think it would be unfair that's why," defended Lawrence. "The lifeguard told me everyone had left the pool when he returned to prepare for the next lap swim session."

"But the drowning occurred on your watch, when everyone was there—including a doctor or two."

"It must have been just an oversight. They simply got out of the water without checking. It could happen to anyone," shrugged Lawrence.

"I still have a story, Mr. Lawrence," said Benjamin. "Unless you figure out a better reason why you didn't sign in swimmers that day and why you weren't ready for emergencies, and why it took so long for help to come. The lifeguard certainly shouldn't have been elsewhere when all this happened. And why was he called away just before this drowning occurred? I'm sure this isn't going to make the club look so great."

With that, Lawrence sighed and sat back in his chair. "What do you want? Ask Doctor Klein she'll verify all this. I've known her for years. Besides she's sort of a specialist and I'm not sure she'd even know CPR or whatever it takes to revive someone as bad off as judge Sims who obviously drowned."

"How long has she been a member of this club?"

"I'm not sure. Lillian here can show you the records. She joined not too long ago. We have people who come and go, of course."

"Does Lillian also have an updated list of the Early Risers swim team?"

"Yes. It's Lillian's job to maintain the list."

"Apparently Lillian doesn't think so. And why didn't you get back to the police when they asked you to?" Benjamin asked.

"How did you know about that?" asked the surprised Lawrence realizing that Kavinsky was the only person checking out such information.

"Cops and reporters kind of hang around together at times, Mr. Lawrence," replied Al, avoiding the disclosure of his source. The manager hesitated, then buzzed his receptionist to come in.

"Lil, I want you to cooperate fully with Mr. Benjamin here. Show him our roster on the Early Risers and any information you may have on Doctor Klein," Lawrence commanded with sweat on his forehead and in a manner apparently over-done to impress the reporter.

Al departed the manager's office after reminding him that he'd be at his newspaper desk shortly and would be available for whatever information he could call him about on this matter. He also mentioned that he'd be going straight to his office after stopping for a car wash enroute for only a few minutes to get some of the mud off his car from his recent hunting expedition.

Benjamin was so concerned about his conversations at the club that he nearly passed by the car wash. It was almost a religious ritual with him to have his car washed at least twice a year—once after the fishing opener and again after pheasant hunting. Otherwise, his old Chev appeared to be the epitome of neglect. And he could care less.

He knew he could get a good deal by filling up at the station with the cylindrical wash and wax buffers. It just happened to be one of Andy Sapel's stations—called "Sapel Six". Sapel owned six of these quickie fill-and-wash sites around Minneapolis. As he drove into the station, he didn't pay any attention to another car, much cleaner and attractive than his, which was following him since he left the club manager.

After gassing up his rusty clunker, he received a receipt at the cashier's desk inside the station's office and got a free wash coupon—minus a wax job—from the unsmiling tough-looking cashier. He thought it strange that the cashier needed Al's name and place of business before giving him the coupon and the receipt listing the numbers to press on the entrance machine to open the doors to the attached car wash shed.

He then went quickly back into the car and got in line behind two other much classier vehicles waiting their turn to enter the closed-door washing facility.

Each wash supposedly took about five minutes. But Al doubted this, since it seemed more like three times that long for the doors to open for him. Upon clicking his wash numbers into the door opener device, he bumped along into the wash area realizing he should someday get some new shocks. The doors closed loudly and tightly behind him. A sign stated that the front door was ready to open only when the light nearby turned green signaling that his car was indeed super clean—at least by "Sapel Six's" standards. This should be quite challenging for the washing system, thought Al.

He closed the windows extra tight, put the car in park, and sat back. Another sign on the wall read: "Relax And Watch The Show." Al was always impressed watching the cylinders start up followed by the whirling of water spray. But he sensed that all this seemed to be making a much louder noise than usual and when they encountered his car the old clunker vibrated more than ever. Al simply thought the mechanism needed some repairs. God knows, he thought, anything that's wrong, Sapel surely has enough money to fix it or even decorate it in gold.

The big cylinder brushes rolled back and forth, on top and around his little car, with the spraying becoming more dense each time they made contact with the car. Al could see the front door, but he could no longer see the back doors or any other object in the car wash for that matter—not even all the signs he previously could see posted along the walls.

He turned the engine off in case that it was creating some of the extra loud noise and checked his vents and air-conditioner to see if they were causing the sudden cloudiness filling the area. The noise kept getting even louder and the mist became so thick that he could barely see anything but steam forming on all his windows.

Al became nervous. Something indeed was happening inside the car wash and he was virtually locked in. Unfortunately, he had no place to run. The doors of his car were so close to the walls he would have difficulty even opening them. The whole environment turned rather eerie. He also sensed a sudden strong odor that seemed to be penetrating into the car. He knew he mustn't become panicky but he wanted to yell for help,although he knew no one could hear him, certainly not the driver in the car outside waiting for the doors to open for the next car wash.

Frustrated and furious, Al also became desperate. He even turned on the window wipers as though they would help him see out. Man, if he ever needed a car phone he needed one now, thought Benjamin. Next, he tried the horn. In fact, he kept blaring the horn intermittently hoping that someone would hear him and come to his rescue. Nothing happened. All he could hear was the continuous spray of whatever it was on his car and the now violent thumping of the cylinder brushes against the vehicle.

The thumping became so violent that his windows began to crack. The cracks spread and finally allowed some of the spray to enter the car causing Benjamin to began coughing incessantly. He began to feel very drowsy, and even though he continued to thump on the car horn and the cleaning mechanism continued at its extremely noisy ear-piercing pitch he feared this wouldn't keep him awake as his eyes began to close.

About all Al could remember at that point was that the exit door had a sign warning that once the car wash was complete drivers should be

CHAPTER 13

Still feeling the results of his bumps and bruises from the car wash, Benjamin, armed with more information, also felt nervous and anxious about finally meeting the mysterious Dr. Klein. He cocked his head and looked in his bathroom mirror with his razor in hand. If he could avoid it, he wouldn't bother shaving his whiskers today. Chances are Dr. Nancy would be pretty casual. His neck and head ached and he thought he felt some pain in his arm, but perhaps he was only imagining all this and was just feeling sorry for himself. He wanted to simply go out the door and be relaxed to face the doctor.and perhaps confront her head-on.

But while bending his arm to attack the whiskers under his chin, he really did feel a tinge of pain—the same type he felt at times when he turned his arm a certain way. He always assumed this was from an accident he suffered while playing touch-football on an Army base in Korea years ago.

Wondering about his arm got him thinking about his upcoming meeting with the doctor. How the hell wa he going to explain the reason for appointment? Maybe he should level with her and get some prescription for the pain. Although he was the only one in the bathroom, he nodded his head that this was a good idea. He nodded too hard, however, and nicked his chin. Wiping the blood away, he thought this would be like killing two birds at one time—entrap the doctor and at the same time get rid of a chronic pain that's been bugging him.

After checking into the newsroom, Benjamin, complete with an oversized Bandaid on his chin, went over his beat assignments posted for the day, shot the breeze with some of his cronies, and left for the garage parking lot to head for the doctor's office. Klein practiced with a group of other neurologists in her downtown Minneapolis office

It took about half-an-hour for Al to find a place to park in the busy ramp adjacent to her medical office building. It was 10 to 10 when he pulled up, and exactly 10 when he finally entered the doctor's office door. He looked as though he may have been punched on the chin.

The receptionist confirming his visit looked at the bandage on his chin as though this was the reason he was there. But to his surprise she simply said, "Oh yes, Dr. Klein is expecting you." To his reporter's mind, this was a bit unusual since he knew most doctors these days have a patient lineup in the waiting room extending almost out the door. With that in mind, he spotted a chair and began catching up on some of his favorite hunting magazines.

However, after flipping only a few pages of an outdoor book with a ferocious bear pictured on the cover, a door opened and a nurse announced that Benjamin should follow here for his appointment. As he guessed, they both stopped at the scales where he was weighed minus his coat and many pens, note paper, glasses and other paraphernalia an old nerdy reporter usually carries about. After noting he was overweight by about 20 pounds, he was led into a little room where he again sat down to read more outdated magazines and stare at Dr. Klein's certificates and other credentials framed on the wall. One certificate especially caught his eye—her maxima cum laude degree from the University of Minnesota.

He stayed seated for nearly an hour and was tempted to call the whole damn visit off when in walked Nancy. He was caught off guard. In his mind, he figured she was too cute to be a doctor. She was a big woman and when she smiled and apologized for the delay he almost forgot why he was there.

When she sat down to put her glasses on, he had all he could do to draw his attention from her legs which he thought were very, very sexy. They were also a bit muscular, Al observed, like someone who works out a lot. It was rather strange that she would wear high heels. Perhaps she wanted to attract as many guys as possible. He changed his gaze quickly to avoid embarrassment and caught her looking at him intently.

"I understand you have some neurological pain Mr. Benjamin?" He unconsciously put his hand to his arm. "Oh yes, I've had this for some time. Usually comes on when I'm shaving or doing some extra work," he said recalling his experience with the razor in the morning.

"Show me where it hurts," she asked, bending closer to his face. Caught somewhat off guard, Benjamin rubbed the top of his shoulder again. "It's been doing that ever since my Army days, doc."

She asked him to take his shirt off and then placed her fingers gently on the spot he pointed to. After a few moments of quiet examination, the doctor took the fingers of his arm and moved them about. Following that she seemed to be checking over parts of his back and neck.

"What kind of work do you do Mr. Benjamin?" asked the lady doctor. "I'm a journalist and I have to use my hands a lot," responded Al quickly, figuring that question was going to come up. "That sounds like an interesting line of work—what do you usually write about?"

"I freelance mostly, write about anything that'll sell—usually publicizing products or services of companies around the area. I interview satisfied customers and prepare case studies on how happy they are with my clients.".

"Oh, I understood you were from the newspaper. Your name sounds so familiar. You're covered by the newspaper's insurance program aren't you?" Al frowned and had to think fast, "Yes, but I do an awful lot of moonlight writing on the side. At the newspaper I usually write only headlines and obits."

"Oh, you're far too humble, Mr. Benjamin, I've seen your by-lines frequently on the front page."

To change the subject, he replied, "I guess I do too much writing—suppose this causes the pain?"

"It could be," she said still looking at him intently. "I'm going to give you some medicine to see how you react. If this doesn't help, let me know in a few weeks and I'll have your shoulder x-rayed."

Sensing she was about to leave before he could know more about her, Benjamin explained to her that he should be more like his friend who went swimming a lot since this probably could work out some of the kinks from his arm. "I understand swimming can do a lot for you, doctor." He then looked closely to study her reaction. She frowned and stared back at him intently as he added, "And I also understand you do lots of it."

"I used to do more when I was younger," she said.

"But I'm told you still do. That you've won a lot of trophies and that you're still a member of some swim club."

He caught a quizzical look on the doctor's face at this point, indicating that he might be coming on too strong. He didn't want this—he wanted to avoid any suspicions or hostilities.

She got up, checked some cabinets, got some pills, and stated: "Try these. However you may have a pinched nerve and you might need some surgery if the pain bothers you too much."

"Thanks doc. I've never gone to a lady doctor before so if I'm a little nervous please overlook it."

"Certainly. I hope I can help you. We seem to have some mutual interests. I write on the side once in a while for some medical trade journals. Your comments about swimming are also quite interesting."

As she put her hand on the door-knob to leave, she asked, "By the way, who is your friend in the swim club?"

Al was waiting for that question. "Was," he corrected. "He was Frank Sims, the judge. Frank was healthy up to the end. I understand he just upped and drowned one morning at the club pool. Shocking. He was always such a good athlete."

The doctor hesitated as though surprised, then continued to open the door. "Yes, I understand. It was a great loss...poor fellow."

The doctor hesitated once more as though wondering what to do next. She turned abruptly, put a hand on Al's shoulder and squeezed it very tightly, surprising the conservative journalist with what he believed to be sort of a come-on. Her hand was strong and brought pain to his shoulder and neck as she applied pressure. She then removed her hand, winked and smilingly reminded him: "Be sure to follow your prescription and let me know how your feel Mr. Benjamin."

With that Al put his shirt back on and returned to the news room still feeling sore from the doctor's grip. Before sitting down at his word processor, however, he noticed a message on his desk to call his nephew. He questioned whether he should mention his doctor visit to Joe since his nephew might be upset over his poking his nose into police matters. He also realized that in some ways he was taking a big risk.

Joe simply wanted to know if the paper had any bio background on the police chief. Al knew what Joe was after without even asking. He told him he'd check out the paper's morgue files for any article on Cermak and try to get a personnel report prepared by the paper and that he'd call him back later in the day.

Benjamin then checked his pocket for his pencil and felt the pills Dr. Klein prescribed. He looked at the label. It read: "For neurological pain...take three times a day before meals."

Being reminded of meals prompted Al to call Joe right back. "What say we do lunch nephew? I got a few more things we can chew on that might interest you."

"Glad you rang. I was just going out the door. How about Jiffy's just down the corner. They've got great burgers but very little ambience." That being resolved, the reporter and detective got together again in a tiny corner of a very busy, but convenient, hamburger joint.

Al avoided mentioning Dr. Nancy and Lawrence for fear of rightfully being scolded for nosing around too much. But he did talk about his call to Dr. Erickson and the strange message left for him by DeSantro that mentioned the name Pelot.

"Who's Pelot?" asked Al. "Is the name pronounced like the French would say it—and have you ever heard of him?" "Haven't the slightest idea who he is," shrugged Joe. "But yeah—it's French, almost sounds like that exotic fruit called Pluot that you can find in the grocery stores these days," Joe chuckled. "But why would he leave you a message?—unless he thought he may not be returning."

"Perhaps Mrs. Sims knows," questioned Al.

"No, and I don't want to ask her," Joe said. "I still don't know if we can trust her, she said she was surprised that anyone thought the judge had any tattoos on him. Hell, sounds like she's never seen her husband with his clothes off.

"Seems to me if she was that distant with her husband, maybe he also kept her far away from his finances. I've been wondering, perhaps the judge had a separate safe that only he knew about. For that matter, he may have some information in there about this guy Pelot or whoever or whatever."

"Do you also suppose the judge had a separate phone away from the missus?" queried Al. "If he was that deceptive he would even be afraid to have her hear any of his special calls."

"Or see them—on his Caller ID monitor," added Joe. "But how in hell do we find the call ID monitor? For that matter, maybe that's why the widow's house was broken into to get it."

Wiping his face with a cheap soiled napkin, Joe concluded, "But look unc, I've gotta go. The chief's piling all kind of work on my desk, and I'm sure it's just to keep me away from getting more involved in this matter. I'll also be gone for awhile and suggest you don't sniff around any more on this unless, of course, you find this so-called secret safe and cell phone," he said with a smile and a bit of sarcasm.

"I still have an ace in the hole," said Al. "The judge's brother Jack and I are good pals. He was the nice Sims. I'll call him again—or go to lunch with him at a decent place," Al added, putting a dig into the crowded little joint they were at. "Maybe he knows of a special phone Caller ID, if there is one, or help find his phone messages the day he drowned."

"Fine unc, but just remember murder is the word—not drowned," corrected Joe.

"When you're dealing with murder, watch your back and be ready to duck. Something like you did at the Sapel gas station only a little bit faster."

He added, "Whoever we're dealing with is slick and wouldn't hesitate to blow you away."

CHAPTER 14

Joe Kavinsky could probably pass off for Don the Beachcomber but certainly not for Tommy Bahama. Decked out in ragged shorts, oversized straw hat, floppy and flimsy beach sandals with long socks and wearing garish colored shades, he added very little class strolling along with stylish Sarah Crimmons through the open shops of Nassau.

However, his intent was to forget all about the pressures up north and just relax and have fun with his very shapely girl friend. Sarah, he mused, could be in even worse clothes than he had on and would still draw lots of attention from admirers, as well as beach bums, on both sides of the road.

His trip, which he informed aunt Kay about just moments before taking off for fear of any interruptions from uncle Al, did have a serious side, however. First of all, he needed some time away from his new sidekick Paulson and Sarah was a very welcome relief. Secondly, his research put Nancy Klein on this island when Dr. DeSantro was there before embarking on his fatal flight to Bimini. He knew, too, that Al was nearly always available, while not on his news rounds, to keep him informed if an emergency came up regarding information on the Sims case.

Although Joe's pants were much too short for any big pockets, he still had room to take along some extra items besides his room key and badge. Besides jingling Bahama coins in one pocket, he carried four snapshots in the other, including those of Dr. Klein, Dr. DeSantro, police chief Cermak, and Zack Crimmons. For some reason, he had a gut feeling that Sarah's father had more to do with this case than meets the eye. In fact, Joe almost sensed Zack was around when he met Frank Meyer. It was like he hired a chaperone to see that no one messes with his little girls.

Unlike in the states, drugs were very much out in the open in the Bahamas. Before he and Sarah walked two blocks down a side road, they were approached by what appeared to be a 12-year-old with a bag of cocaine stuffed in his shirt. "Hey mon, wan' some high for you and girl?"

"How mucho muchacho?" asked Joe in his worst, broken Spanish.

"Naw, mon, I speak English—most of us do. Only four bucks, mon, and you get all this," replied the scraggly looking lad sticking out a hand with some packaged white substance.

"We'll pass, son," shrugged the cop. "And if I were you I'd throw it in the ocean and start doing your homework"

This didn't phase the young pusher who kept his fixed smile and approached another couple coming down the road.

"Oh Joe, that poor little guy. He should be playing baseball or something, not selling narcotics. How and why do kids turn out like this?" sighed Sarah looking sadly up at her muscular but very sun-burned escort.

"If you know the answer tell the world, Sarah, especially around here. Some of the natives are running rampant with it. They drive the narcs in Miami nuts. It's almost impossible to keep the stuff from coming to the states. They get there any which way, boat, inner tube, you name it."

After purchasing a few trinkets from a straw shop, Joe and Sarah found an outdoor café to catch a snack and try to figure things out. Despite the carefree setting, however, Sarah could note that her boyfriend was very deep in thought at times.

"You're still wondering about the Sims case, I can tell," quizzed Sarah smiling and touching a finger to his frowning forehead.

"Yep. It's a good thing you remembered Nancy Klein from your school days. If it wasn't for your friends telling you where Nancy hung out on these islands I never would have pin-pointed it to this vicinity. Hell, it could have been miles down the road in Freeport. I guess she took plenty of wild spring breaks our here."

He continued softly, as though talking to himself, "she was the number two person…but who was the number one?"

"What on earth do you mean, Mr. detective?" asked Sarah still smiling but taking note of his sudden seriousness.

"I mean who was the swimmer who took Sims' key from around his neck, and why?—and was that the same guy who was suppose to take it?" Joe continued, "A series of numbers were found between his toes by the assistant coroner who then left the country. He said he informed Sims' wife about all this, but she told me she knew nothing about it—nor any mysterious key.

"But how could a wife not know about her husband's tattoos, no matter how small?" He then mumbled,thoughtfully, "Perhaps Doc DeSantro fled to Central America—Colombia for instance—to either collect payment from a bank with his special key and safe-deposit numbers.or make payment with laundered money he got from Nassau for more drugs. He added,"For that matter, he may have been flying back to Nassau to celebrate his good fortune with his friend Nancy. She in turn then may have substituted his case of money with a suitcase full of bombs as he took off again to deal with a drug kingpin like, maybe, Robert Beck who I understand is hiding in Bimini. Hell, She may have figured the money would buy her even a bigger fortune in drugs if flown to the good old Twin Cities."

"Whew and whoa—you're going much too fast for me," broke in Sarah. "Do that one more time…only this time come up for air quicker."

Joe chuckled, knowing he was being carried away by it all. "Somehow, Sarah, I think I got all the pieces, but the one big piece I haven't yet figured out is the guy or gal who the judge met first while swimming in that pool. And how does the police chief fit into all this—and where does Sapel fit into this picture?"

She stopped him with a quick question of her own. "Speaking of pictures, why are you fumbling with those snapshots? One looks like daddy."

"Yep," admitted the cop, taking a deep breath to gather more of his thoughts on the subject.

Joe lit a cigarette and blew some smoke as if to relax, while Sarah continued to look at him quizzically for an explanation. "Look honey, I'm not out after your father. I'm just trying to get some answers to a mystery that keeps unraveling. At this point in my mind I'm not excluding anyone from being involved. I don't think the Arab world is, since the islands around here are much more convenient and conducive to such drug transactions. But I could be wrong, dead wrong."

"I've never really been able to know my father," Sarah said with a frown. "He's been like a mystery himself. When he and mom split, Susan and I were sort of on our own. Mom was all wrapped up emotionally and went off the deep end trying to get even and just to keep going with the kids and her life.

"I never could figure out if all the threats she had from daddy were real or just make believe to turn Susan and I off from him. But she did have some very good reasons to mistrust him."

She added with a frown, "I remember he was gone an awful lot. We often wondered where and why and my mom even wondered. Both Susan and I could see the divorce coming, although mom was very fearful of the consequences.

"Daddy would be gone a lot with his business associates. Sometimes he'd take Susan and me shopping after he got back and would buy us fabulous gifts, almost anything we'd want, telling us he struck it rich while he was gone.

"But when he left mom, we very seldom saw him again unless it was by way of a postcard from some distant place or a gift on the holidays."

Kavinsky snubbed out his cigarette. "Let me put it this way honey. Your dad may be more involved in this than we want to believe. Once you get in with the drug network it's awfully hard to pull out."

"If I know my father at all, Joe, I can truly say he's not a killer."

"I hope you're right. But there's all ways of killing—some direct some indirect. In the drug world, it's tough to figure out one from the other. The bottom line is all that counts for coke heads. If you get in the way of someone making big bucks you're history."

Sarah interrupted, "You still didn't tell me what you're doing with those pictures. I have a suspicion that you're not down here for just fun and games Joe."

"Mostly so," promised Joe. "As long as we're here, though, let's do some snooping in the area where Nancy Klein may have met DeSantro. I'd like to ask some of the folks here if they've ever seen her or anyone she may have been hanging around with during her visits."

"And that's where the pictures fit in?"

"Right. Maybe I can show them around between sun tanning and romance."

However, Joe and Sarah found little time for either during the remainder of that afternoon. They must have visited more than a dozen spots, including more straw shops, travel counselors, hotels, resorts and bars, asking those in charge if they recognized any of those in the photos. Finally, somewhat in frustration, they reconnoitered during a happy hour in the lobby of one of Nassau's finer watering holes.

"What do you say to finishing off this day with a trip to Paradise Island?" suggested Joe. "I hear there's lots of things to do there—play a little in the casinos, take in a show, do a little hanky panky…?"

"Sounds like just what we need," agreed Sarah, reaching out to touch Joe's hand holding his drink. "I guess Merv Griffin invested lots of money over in Paradise but now other big financiers are building greater things onto it."

'Yeah, and there's a lot left to be done—especially on the black jack tables," added Joe looking at his watch. "There's one huge hotel-resort called Atlantis that puts Vegas to shame—but we better figure on doing it now."

Sarah put on her most provocative evening dress and dangling earrings to be escorted out by the dashing young police lieutenant for a night on nearby Paradise Island. A cab took them the approximate 11 miles to reach Paradise, going over a long one-way bridge spanning Shirley Street. The cab ride provided a panoramic view of the busy harbor below where giant cruise ships mingled with the U.S. Navy fleet, as if calmly awaitng the return of their excited sightseeing passengers. All seemed drawn to the glitter of the towers of Atlantis and the eye-catching mecca of a myriad of busy resorts and shops.

They chose one of the most fancy eating places in the Atlantis to dine and wine, selecting a special Bahamian seafood combination and a strange after dinner liqueur recommended by a big jolly Bahamian waiter. After this, they were soon on their way to the bright lights and jingling slot machines in the many casinos and variety of entertainment spots where they tried the slots, threw dice and played cards. But they soon realized having fun in Paradise Island can be rather pricey.

Upon losing many chips on the blackjack tables and cashing in some won on roulette, Joe and Sarah decided to do the tango at the Bahamian Club and catch the revue at the nearby LeCabaret.

After seeing the topless ladies cavorting with their males dancers in tight pants on stage, embarrassing even Joe, some steel drum music started Sarah snapping her fingers with the beat. Following this was a second-rate magician and a rather clumsy tumbler. It was near closing time when they tried their luck again at the casino. But it wasn't long before the cop had to dig even deeper into his wallet. This time, in so doing, some of the photos he had been carrying about earlier in the day fell out of the wallet accidentally.

"Hey mon, you know Nancy?"

Both Joe and Sarah spun around to catch a big smiling black face looking over their shoulders at one of the fallen photos. The fella speaking was wearing a chauffeur's cap and had just picked up some of the photos from the floor.

"Do you know her, pal?" quizzed the cop.

"Sure mon—my name's Dingy. She hangs out here at times. Nancy Fredricks—plays the tables a lot. A pretty lucky lady, too."

"Are you a friend of hers?" asked Sarah excitedly.

"I've driven her around sometimes in my limo. She's a good tipper when she's winning, but mean when she's losing.She's usually with lots of company," recalled the large fellow.

"When did you see her last?" inquired Joe.

"Oh, about a month ago. She usually stays over at the Marriott Nassau Resort on Cable Beach when she comes with her friends."

"Is this one of her friends?" asked Kavinsky showing the picture of Dr. DeSantro.

"Yeah mon—I've seen that guy somewhere before."

"Was he with her the last time you picked her up Dingy?"

"Yep—he and a bearded guy they called Pelot. But why so many questions mon?"

"Pelot? Tell me more about Pelot," Joe eagerly inquired ignoring Dingy's question. His expression showed his surprise at the sound of this name, the same name his uncle mentioned while recently talking about this drug case. He picked up on it immediately, even though Dingy didn't pronounce it in the same French way as Al would. "Where did he come from and why was he with Nancy?" asked Joe. With this, the black man frowned and backed off somewhat.

Knowing that this was a sign when some incentive may need to be offered, Joe smiled and gently suggested "Friend, may I buy you a drink over there for a few minutes of your time," pointing to a nearby bar and flashing some bills. Eyeing the money, the bow-tied driver, grinning again, replied "Sure mon, but I may not have many answers."

Purchasing drinks, Joe and Sarah then ushered their new-found friend to a cocktail table surrounded by several stools in a corner away from the bar, far removed from the loud noise and occasional hilarious laughter coming from the gambling parlor.

After introducing themselves, they learned that their friendly informer went by the full name of "Dingy Richards"—a native of CAP Island in the Bahamas, which he proudly noted was the birthplace of the famous actor Sydney Poitier. Dingy knew most of the surrounding islands like the back of his hands, especially Paradise where he lived for many years. Joe slipped him a twenty after drink orders were taken and pumped him further about DeSantro and Klein—or, as Dingy called her, "Miss Fredricks." He knew DeSantro as simply Ray.

"Did you drive these two to the airport?" asked Joe. The cheerful black man took another sip of his drink, wiped his mouth with his hand and frowned as if getting more serious. "Seems to me there were three people, mon. That guy Pelot was with them."

"Did they have a suitcase?"

"Yeah, I tried to help Ray with it—it was very heavy. But he only wanted Nancy to help."

Was there only one?" probed Joe. Dingy, apparently distracted by one of the shapely waitresses strolled by, slowly replied "one suitcase?"

"Yeah, was there just one suitcase?" Joe tried to control his patience and emotions and lowered his voice, realizing that Dingy wasn't being arrested and that his training as a cop sometimes made him too commanding and intimidating in his questioning.

"The lady had a parcel too. It looked like a large purse, if that's what you're asking," said Dingy with a shrug of his broad shoulders.

"Did you wait for her to get back in your cab after she dropped him off?"

"Yeah, mon—they gave me an extra five to stay around for awhile."

The conversation was now leading somewhere, Kavinsky thought. He took a drink, smiled at Sarah, and then looked hard at Dingy. "Now think about this carefully Dingy before answering—did the lady return with the suitcase?"

The jovial driver became somewhat somber again with the stern look from the cop. He scratched his balding head and squinted his eyes as though deeply pondering the question. Joe impatiently asked, "can you remember anything about this?"

"No problem mon. I think she did come back with a suitcase. I remember helping her put it in the trunk. It was very heavy for the lady, although she seemed quite strong."

"Did it look like the very same case—was it the same color and the same size?" quizzed Joe.

"I think it was. But it's hard to remember what happened a month ago. I do know though mon that she had more than that little handbag with her when she returned.'"

To stimulate the conversation, Joe slipped another twenty in the big fella's hand.

"Thanks Dingy. Just one more question, do you remember where you dropped Pelot off after the airport trip?"

After some hesitation, the chauffeur snapped his fingers and said, "Yeah, mon, I remember he must be a banker. It was in a ritzy part of town where most of the bankers live." He paused, then recalled, "It must have been his place but the sign out front didn't say Pelot. It said McNeil or McNair—some Irish name. That's it—McNair."

Before Dingy could ask who Joe was or represented, the couple put a tip on the table and waived farewell as they went out the door and once more into the crowd of peddlers and tourists.

"What was all that about?" asked Sarah, somewhat amused over Joe's questioning.

"It could mean that our friend Nancy returned with DeSantro's bag of money. Somehow she did pull off a switch leaving him believe he was flying out to Bimini with his loot."

"Now I just have to figure out what happened in the airport that out-foxed the doc. Maybe this guy Pelot helped. Or another so-called friend met them and changed suitcases so the doc got the bomb."

"But Joe—what a terrible friend. Who do you think would do such a thing?"

"Dunno—suppose it had to be someone so close to the two of them that DeSantro had no suspicions," theorized the cop. "Maybe someone in the medical examiner's office," he added as Sarah leaned her head on his arm and said, "maybe your uncle knows, honey, he covers that beat." Joe agreed.

"Yeah, he sure doesn't like the head ME, Ed Loring. They've had some run-ins lately. I don't have a cell phone, but I'll call unc to see if there was someone else from Loring's office over here at the time. Whoever it was may have made off with all the laundered cash."

They caught the number 10 bus direct to Cable Beach since number 9 stopped too often in the run-down areas of Nassau and was usually so filled that many passengers had to sit in the aisle. Before retiring, he and Sarah had a night cap at Dickey Moe's restaurant and visited an off-the-road joint called the Zoo. It was really swinging and Joe got his legs all tangled up again dancing, trying to keep up with what the natives call jamming. They had to cover their ears at times when the steel drums were beating. Joe also got the message that Sarah, checking her watch, was ready to cuddle up for the night.

Spending the rest of the night with Sarah was sensational for Kavinsky. The closeness of her body was indescribable for Joe who wasn't much for words anyway, especially in this situation. As he kissed her soft warm lips he noticed a smile on her face as though, indeed, he was also something special for her. He couldn't explain why, but he suddenly felt much more than just passion for this woman. He realized now more than ever that his entire being was truly alive with an intense, burning desire for making Sarah his possession, his and his only, and of forever protecting her. Unlike others, she wasn't just something to make love to and leave.

She was indeed truly his—they belonged to one another. This feeling confirmed a genuine commitment between them and kept interrupting the ecstasy of the moment. It was a newcomer in Joe's love-making that he wasn't sure he wanted until now. But it remained and eventually engulfed his whole being—as though telling him that their love was forever here to stay.

And he knew, without need for words, that the woman in his clutches was having the same feelings. Her breathing and emotion were more exciting and intense than ever as both seemed to have a combining of thoughts as well as of bodies to make their love even more complete.

It wasn't until sunshine peeked through the worn curtains that both realized morning had arrived. But the entrance of day-break was different this time. Without expressing the exhilaration of the night, they were aware that both indeed had fallen very much in love—deeply as well as passionately—during those past few hours in the semi darkness of their hotel room.

In showering, dressing, even at breakfast in the small off-street breakfast nook that they strolled to, hand-in-hand, across from their hotel, they were one together and wishing to remain attached eternally. They were blissfully content in knowing that they were really united in how they felt for one another. This was definitely "it" thought Joe, no more flitting around with every girl he could wink at.

Sarah broke the wonderful silence as they gazed at each other. "Darling, don't you want to call your uncle?"

Her words brought him back to his real world, although he knew he was out of character in this world of committed love that he was daydreaming about so much. "Yes—dammit! I almost forgot," he said putting a napkin to his face and glancng at his watch.

"I guess this is a good time to catch him in as any—almost Sunday afternoon back home. I'm sure he'll be ready to turn on the Vikings football game."

He knew Al's phone number like the back of his hand, which is why he was so sure he didn't dial wrong when no one answered right away. But realizing the many miles of water separating him from home, he remained patient as the ringing continued. Al, he thought, will be really mad if this interrupts watching his game, especially if the Vikes are scoring or, most likely, being sacked.

He finally heard what seemed to be a noise at the other end. "Uncle Al, Aunt Kay…are you there?" He waited a second or two until a very feeble, nearly inaudible reply came back.

"Joey—is that you?"

Kavinsky was sure he had a terrible phone connection "I can hardly hear you, uncle Al…you sound so weak Are you okay? Are the Vikings winning?"

But he didn't get the wise-cracking response he expected. "I dunno— I've been in bed Joey. Guess I've been having the flu or something. It's been coming on for a few days or so.

Where are ya?" asked Al.

"Sorry to hear that, unc. I'm in the Bahamas. Took a little time off from that pressure cooker up there."

"You doing any good?" He sensed at once that his uncle knew he was snooping around in detective work and probably with some woman.

"I think I'm getting some good information for us on the Sims case, but don't let anyone know up there unc."

To Joe's surprise, he didn't get any reaction, nothing—not even a cough. Al must really be out of it, he figured. To get more response, he got directly to the point.

"Look uncle Al. Do me a big favor. I'm playing a hunch, okay? Find out, if you can, if anyone from Doc DeSantro's medical examiner's office was in the Bahamas on the days he was suppose to be gone on vacation—or if anyone in his office was out of the country anywhere during that time."

He still didn't get the quick reaction he expected. After a long pause, Al mumbled, "Oh—okay Joe. Give me your number and I'll get back to you. Hope I can shake this soon."

"Unc, I need to know real soon. If you can do it, let me know by tomorrow afternoon. I'll still be at the Marriott—101-202-7896. Okay? Say hello to aunt Kay and take care of yourself. If I don't hear from you by mid week, I'll call you back…I may be going to Bimini later in the week."

Joe expected at least a goodbye from the other end, but all he heard was a click,indicating that Al must have hung up. He was surprised, but figured that long distance caused some problems at times and that his uncle would be coming through for him, as he always has, in a big way. You could count on him.

Sarah knew of Joe's plans to visit Bimini by now and realized she had only one more day to vacation with her lover. The two of them spent the remaining time strolling along the beaches, hitting the shops and otherwise just forgetting about the troubles of the world.

But she knew, too, what Joe may be running into at Bimini—that a cop probing around a drug lord's back yard may be pushing his luck too far. She also realized she couldn't talk him out of it—and that he was doing this not only for the good of innocent folks in and around the Twin Cities but also out of duty and, of course, for her—and for her mom. She smiled at this thought.

Over the next night and into the afternoon prior to departure, they both kept communicating, by word and action, of their deep love for one another. They were hardly able to break away from their embraces long enough to pack for their separate evening flights. And it was only then that Joe began to wonder when, and if, he would be hearing from Al Benjamin.

They left Cable Beach early to allow time for Joe to make a call from the airport. Check-in was quick despite the departure and custom lines formed by tourists coming and going. Joe and Sarah waited on a bench, hand-in-hand, for the time their separate flights would depart. The Bimini flight would be only a few minutes in the air, and Sarah should be back in Miami on a direct

American Airlines flight in less than an hour. In only several more hours she'd be back in Minneapolis.

Thinking of goodbyes seemed to push everything else from the cop's mind until he spotted a phone booth as he was once again planting a kiss on Sarah's beautiful lips. "Damn!—uncle Al, I forgot to call him" he uttered. But then again, he remembered, wasn't Al suppose to call him?

Joe became rather flustered, especially when he saw the gang of people in line waiting to use the airport phone near him. Luckily, Sarah had her cell phone in her purse. Dialing hastily, he reached a wrong number which only made more upset. His second try, however, got through to Al's wife—this time very clearly.

Kay informed him that his uncle was in bed, still feeling quite ill—probably from that flu going around at the newspaper office. She said Al was able to get about that day and left Joe a message if he called. Before Joe could ask what the message said, Kay volunteered: "It's short and brief, Joe. He said to tell you that it was Loring. He was in Nassau the day the plane crashed and that Sims' brother searched the judge's cell phone memory system and the name Pelot was still on it Fortunately, some of the judge's notes were stuffed, almost hidden, inside a table drawer near his bed. They revealed that Pelot is really a guy by the name of John C. McNair of the International Canadian Bank."

Joe thanked his aunt and hung up thoughtfully. "So Loring's in on this, too. They're doing their dirty money laundering at his bank," he concluded. It all came together now, he figured, Pelot and Nancy apparently wanted to prevent Sapel from sharing in the drug profits. The judge had numbers on him that, if combined with those on Pelot's phone message, would be the combination to get drug money from the bank. Loring, at the request of Sapel, probably was in the Bahamas to observe the switch but wasn't aware that Pelot and Nancy deposited the loot into the bank. Sapel must have been furious when he didn't get his share and blamed Loring for screwing up the entire plan.

But Joe had no time to figure who else was involved since he had to get back to Sarah to get ready for his hop to the tiny airport of the narc king in a corner of Bimini. As planned, he first entered a nearby restroom and went into one of the stalls, making sure to latch it. He sat on the stool and took out a wallet, removing a passport. Although it's not required to have one entering the Bahamas, some photo identification is. He figured an old Army ID photo and some phony passport should get him by.

Joe reached into another pocket for what appeared to be a combination stamp and pliars with a large flat head. The top of this strange tool was circular and revolved when the cop turned to the words he needed and pressed the jaws of this apparatus onto a page of the passport. It clearly stamped the name Joseph P. Barrott on the page and showed Joe's face. An official looking passport stamp was registered onto the page—just like those used to walk through customs around the world.

"Voila!" he whispered without the proper accent upon seeing the impressive result. His confidence in police tricks was renewed. He then removed all personal identification in his tacky wallet and flushed them down the toilet, replacing them with his new revised passport along with his unnamed service photos.

On his way to rejoin Sarah, he noticed another wall phone. This gave him the idea to try calling McNair. It would be tough to trace an anonymous call from a pay phone. Besides, the call letting McNair know that someone was on to the mysterious Pelot would be quite upsetting to the entire drug/bank network. With that in mind, Joe dialed the bank after looking up the number in the worn old phone book hanging nearby. But when he asked to speak to McNair he was put on hold. After checking his watch several times, a voice finally said: "We're sorry sir, but Mr. McNair passed away a few weeks ago."

"What happened?" was all Joe could ask, somewhat shaken by surprise. "He was struck crossing the road near the Bahama development building at Cable Beach appparently by a hit-and-run driver." But Joe sensed that the banker was killed for knowing too much. In fact, the killer may have already drawn out the drug money from the bank and was eluding the mad and greedy Minnesota mob. He simply hung up, leaving no message.

Joe returned to Sarah shaking his head over the increasing complexity of this case. His farewell to Sarah was exciting to behold by passersby. He kissed her emotionally for a least half-a-minute before reminding her" "If anyone asks, I stopped off in Miami for a few days. I sure hope I remember my new name—Joseph Barrott. Shouldn't be a problem though—I'll just answer to my old handle of Joe."

"You haven't forgotten anything?" she asked wrinkling her cute little forehead.

"Not even my gun," replied Joe tapping his pocket. He then planted another kiss on his beloved to let her know he certainly wasn't about to forget her—ever.

CHAPTER 15

Kavinsky's gun was somewhat unusual, to say the least. It looked as small as a derringer, but it was much more powerful and could be broken down into many parts. He learned about this potent little weapon in police academy, as well as how to separate the parts so it would be virtually impossible to detect even through the best of airport X-ray machines.

He hardly had time to double-check his few belongings on the quick trip to the tiny airstrip, almost hidden away in an area bordered by palm trees. The flight was in a vintaged 12-place prop-jet—probably the same type DeSantro was a passenger on. Despite the bumpy ride and overcast conditions, he was able to get a glimpse of the islands of Bimini from a few miles out and noted that they were indeed all by themselves, northwest of another lonely piece of land called Andros. A few beacon lights from a little patch of ground on the smaller and less populated of the islands helped the pilot of the shaky airplane find the landing spot which was almost completely surrounded by water.

Upon landing, Kavinsky followed the others to a small counter, a make-shift customs site. A somewhat scruffy young black man also with a baseball cap and big smile greeted the new arrivals. Several other big black guys stood nearby and the cop sensed they were around to take care of troublemakers—whoever they may be.

"Hello mon, and where might you be from?" welcomed the strange-looking customs official. "You and me are baseball players," he said with a big grin, looking at Joe's Minnesota Twins cap and pointing to his Phillies cap which was on backwards. "Are you from the land of our godfather—Adam Clayton Powell?"

Joe was at first lost for words. But he quickly recalled that Powell was once a controversial U.S. Congressman who spent his final days putting together a colony of followers on these islands. With that he extended his hands and slapped his palms together with those of the young black in high-five style.

'I'm from northern Minnesota, man. Joe Barrott is the name and construction is my game."

"Okay Joe. Anything in the bags I should see?" Kavinsky knew he meant drugs or guns.

"Naw, I'm clean—too clean. There's no work where I'm from. Need some money to play with. Hope to do a few odd jobs around here and head for the casinos."

"Only work I know of around here is up on poppa's hill," said the customs guy. "You know anyone up there?"

"Not really. But I'm willing to learn."

The smile faded from the young black's face as he signaled the two brawny guys behind him. Kavinsky felt nervous as the two muscle men approached and studied his passport and photos.

"Sorry mon, but we must also search your belongings."

Joe knew he mustn't hesitate nor let his nervousness show. "Sure, go right ahead.—You gotta do whatcha gotta do, right?"

The big fellows indicated that he should follow them, after easily picking up his bags from the floor next to the counter. They led him into a small room where there were only two chairs and a small table.

"Strip down, please," the larger man with a mustache demanded.

"You mean everything?"

'To your shorts," said the one with the glasses.

Joe quickly followed orders, even taking off his socks. They then opened his bags and took out each of the few items he packed, including a small radio, camera, extra set of jogging shoes, and other numerous and uninteresting paraphernalia.

Following that ritual, they checked over his pants, shirt pocket, socks, and even peeked in his shorts while he was standing.

"What the hell you guys looking for?" he finally asked.

"Just standard procedure when someone comes in looking for work around here, mon," explained the mustached one.

'Put your stuff back on, mon. You look clean enough, he declared," adding "but you gotta leave your camera with us 'till you're off the islands, which you must be after three months if you're not employed. So you better hustle."

To avoid conflict over his camera, Joe responded, "thanks fellas. I'll keep that in mind. Now if you'll give me back my belongings I'll be on my way. Incidentally, I'll be back for the camera. It's got the name Joe with a heart inscribed on it for my girl friend.'

They opened the door as one of the more beefy guards inquired, "By the way, mon, where you staying?"

"At the Pilot Knob motel."

"Good. Just so we know where to get ya if we hafta come looking."

When Joe was alone, he made sure all his items were intact and headed out up the hill to town. The many pebbles and rocks along the dirt road were an extra burden as he trudged up the narrow path in his extra large work shoes. Although Bimini is modern in some areas, this wasn't one of them.

The need to appear down-on-his luck, without fare for even a cab ride to the motel, was important to Joe since he was aware that many eyes may still be on him even as he made his way farther from their binoculars. He walked with his bags to a small gas station, where he borrowed a key to the gent's rest room. Once inside he found little time to observe the filth and graffiti around him as he made a point to latch the door.

He then quickly opened a bag and removed what appeared to be a metal bar from its inside frame. He next opened the back of his transistor radio and removed a tiny clip and trigger attachment, which at first looked like part of the inner workings of the radio. After that, he bent down to slide back the thick sole of one of his shoes, revealing 20 small caliber bullets squeezed side-by-side under the sole.

Kavinsky hurriedly put all the parts together, placed the bullets in the cartridge, and jammed the clip into the compact pistol handle. He then carefully placed the pistol in the special small compartment of the sole, turned on the water, slapped a few drops on his face and flushed the toilet to sound like he was using it in case someone had an ear to the door

He made his exit to the nearby road again after dropping off the key with the attendant and asking for the location of the Pilot Knob. The walk to the old motel wasn't as far away as he expected. In fact, the airport was only a few miles from town. The Pilot Knob was on a side street, two-stories, and very unkempt—just the type humble setting Joe desired to avoid suspicion. And he knew from research, that he was now close to the estate and private airstrip of the notorious drug lord Robert Beck.

Upon checking into his tiny room, Kavinsky could see from his window the few lights of what must be main street and could hear the sound of traffic coming mostly from what appeared to be the busy brothels around the corner. He tried to close the window but found that it was fixed in place, probably from rust and old age, and resigned himself to having one hell of a time getting a good night sleep in this flea trap.

However, he was surprised to be awakened by a rooster crowing than by road noise. He scratched his head and figured he slept soundly through the night. At first he wondered if he was on sort of a farm, but looking at his watch discovered that morning had indeed arrived and the rooster was at a nearby shed announcing the sunrise. His watch also informed him also that he actually overslept.

Still drowzy, Joe wasn't too sure where he really was at first. When reality caught up with him, he quickly jumped out of the soiled covers as though creepy crawlers were after him. He avoided shaving and applying deodorant and after brushing his teeth and dressing, put his belongings back in his bags and headed toward the first place that looked like it might serve coffee.

Finding a stool around the breakfast counter, the cop sat down, lit a cigarette and blew smoke out calmly while assessing his new surroundings. After a few swigs of coffee, he spotted a corner equipped with a bus stand sign and figured this may be the start for his trip to Beck's.

Joe lucked out. He waited only a few minutes before an old rusty bus pulled up with the markings: "Beck Bus." Upon boarding, the driver motioned for him to sit down and drove off before he could find change to pay him. "No need," said the driver noticing that Joe looked like a typical American struggling to get change and stay erect while the bus lurched forward. He nearly fell into a seat and began looking out a window wondering where all his fellow passengers were bound.

In only a few minutes, after a bumpy ride through mostly desolate countryside, the bus came to a small guard station, where the uniformed attendant stepped out with an official looking check-in pad. No words were spoken. The guard simply walked to the bus, opened the door and peered inside as though counting the number of passengers.

Kavinsky felt tense, despite the somewhat lazy attitude of everyone around him. He was hoping that the miniature gun in the sole of his shoe would go unnoticed. However, he could feel the pressure of it already on the arch of his foot and was worried that he might start limping and give away his little secret. Apparently satisfied with his inspection, the guard took a pencil out, made some marks on the sheet, and signaled the driver to move on. Wherever the bus was headed, Joe was getting both confused and even amused by this entire amateur, almost laughable, security system in progress.

His curiosity and interest increased, however, when the bus proceeded into an area where many people, apparently workers, were busy doing everything from mechanical repairs to shop keeping. All of this activity seemed to surround his primary area of interest, however, which took the form of a long and narrow airport runway and hangars.

There was a great mixture of buildings, mostly shacks, around the entire area. One of these, a more stable type structure, was where the bus finally pulled up and stopped. A large, roughly painted and misspelled sign reading: "Pirsonel" caught the cop's eyes immediately upon getting off the bus. All of the shabby looking travelers entered the building so Joe followed along. They encountered a small waiting line, with many just standing around with their wide cowboy hats or dozing with heads resting on bended knees while sitting on the dirty floor.

The cop was glad he brought enough cigarettes to while-away the time since he feared this could take a few hours at the least. But the line seemed to move faster than he expected and within the first hour he was almost at the entrance to the door of the personnel office, behind which all the activity apparently took place.

What kind of activity, he wasn't sure, but he felt it must have some connection to the hiring of workers for the Beck operations and that he was lucky to have caught a bus load of folks who were also looking for work there. He noticed that the doors were closed shut and loudly locked each time a person entered and that no one came out those doors, which were always opened by the same attendant.

After a few more puffs on his cigarette, Joe was called into the mysterious room behind the door and asked to sit and face two very tough looking fat guys with big sombreros.

"Que tal, senior," greeted the white guy on the left. "Hable usted espanol?" Joe knew enough about basic Spanish that this meant hello and can you speak Spanish to reply simply, "no senior."

"Ah, then you probably aren't Cuban or Mexican and can speak American, as we prefer to use," commented the smiling black man on the right. "Do you have your papers to work here?"

"Just my passport, no one told me to bring anything else at customs," shrugged Joe, a bit angry at himself for not checking into this.

With that he handed the black man the phony passport. Flipping it to the page with the latest stamp, both men behind the desk looked it over quietly and then gave it back to a nervous Joe.

"You are a long way from here, Mr. Barrott—am I pronouncing it right?" When Joe nodded yes, he continued, "We know about Minnesota—we do a lot of business there. Why do you wish to work here?"

"I know some friends who knew poppa Powell. They told me I could make some quick money here and maybe go on to find some more work dealing cards in Nassau or Freeport."

"Ah, so you're a card dealer, mon," declared the white guy. "Well, the only deals here are those you have to work hard for."

'That's what I want—work and plenty of it."

The two interrogators looked at one another. The black man then said with a frown, "But first you have to be examined—a test—to see if you fit in with Mr. Beck's work."

After a brief, thoughtful silence, Joe responded, "What kind of a test?"

"A test where we ask all the questions, mon," the frowning one replied holding up the palm of his hand to stop Joe from continuing any further inquiries.

"First of all, you must go through our x-ray station," he said point-ing, to another x-ray checkout site located in an adjoining room exposed by an open door. "Then you must fill out some more papers."

"And then?" asked Joe, risking some more palm-halting by the guy leading the questioning.

"And then we tell you if Mr. Beck wants you," shrugged the cocky white guy.

The cop was then led into the x-ray room and told to strip to his shorts. "I did this all at customs," Joe shrugged. He then said, "Excuse me, but my feet are killing me with these old shoes. I'll take these off, too." Not hearing any argument, he carefully removed his shoes, placed them in a special non-magnetic bag, and carried them through the x-ray device. He was greatly relieved that no signals went off as he strolled past, pretending to be as unconcerned as possible. One of the more muscular fellows was busy checking over his clothing with a bar while the other watched his progress. But Joe felt his gut getting tense when the clothes-checker turned his gaze at Kavinsky's dirty shoes.

Just by luck, a plane nearly buzzed the building at that instance and made such a noise that everyone instinctively ducked. "Those damn drug runners—most of them don't even know how to fly a plane," grumbled the black man. "Maybe they're flying too high," chuckled Joe attempting to divert their attention away from his shoes.

"Don't try to be funny, Mr. Barrott—This is a very serious business," said the would-be shoe checker as he beckoned the next guy in line to be examined, apparently forgetting about Joe's shoes. Kavinsky took a deep breath and almost blessed himself.

Motioning Joe to move on, the black fella said, "Here are our papers, fill them out in the next room." As the cop put on his pants and shoes, he asked, "When do I start?" This annoyed the white guy, "You'll know soon enough," he said waving his hand for Kavinsky to move on. "We have many others to see. Just follow the others, ask no more questions, and you may be given an employee time card," added his grumpy companion.

Joe began to relax as he sat back at the bench where he started this process. Like the others he began checking over the form he had to fill out. It was somewhat similar to any other work application form, except it asked if he was on drugs and how he felt about drug pushing. But most of the questions required simply a yes or no.

He didn't hesitate answering the drug questions either since he marked down exactly what they would like to see, pretending he was a junkie as well as a pusher. And he was glad at this point that he scratched his arm with a needle while in Nassau, even though it still hurt like hell.

Going without lunch didn't seem to bother any of the folks riding with him from the personnel site. However, Joe was sorry now that he didn't add a pancake or two to his breakfast to hold him over for the next exciting incident. But nothing much happened for the remainder of the day, since the cop was simply transported to a quonset hut where he was told that everyone passed their "tests" and would now be housed at this beat-up old structure near the airport hangar while working for Beck.

Joe didn't hang around with most of the others in the hut, who were busy chatting in what seemed to be Cuban lingo. Instead, he began walking around the area to see what kind of digs drug lord Beck developed since leaving the U.S. with the narcs hot on his trail more than a decade or so ago.

However, he only got a few blocks from the hut before a Jeep with several uniformed, mean-looking hombres stopped him to see his credentials. Fortunately, he took his official looking credential card along from the personnel boys,but he still was soundly scolded by the guy in the passenger seat who told him emphatically, in both Spanish and English, that he was never allowed to stroll around the premises without a security guy at his side.

Upon returning to the hut, he recalled some of the sights he observed. One was a large assortment of expensive houses, some that looked like mansions that were fenced off and protected by pistol-packing. dudes at guard stations. The other was the barricaded private airstrip next to the largest mansion in the area.

Within a short time after Joe claimed his cot and clothes hangars his group was told to meet in the nearby mess hall for chow. While hanging up his few items and placing his other shoes and bag under the bed, a young man with a beard introduced himself. His name was Charley. He, too, was from the Midwest—Michigan—and appeared to be the only one who didn't speak Cuban. A very muscular fellow, he had a broad smile and wanted to be very friendly, exceptionally so, thought Joe.

He and his new chum ate together, a few chairs away from the others. Charley, it seemed, had a drug problem and had gotten into lots of trouble with the law back home. He felt that Bimini allowed him to do his thing and at the same time gave him the chance to get a job and pay for his habit without risking jail. He grew up in the U.S., joined the Navy at 17, but was discharged before graduating from boot camp when marijuana showed up in his blood stream. His folks gave up on him and he was on a downer ever since.

Joe had his biography all memorized so he could readily relate it to anyone asking. He told Charley he was a high school dropout who became unemployed in Minnesota's hard-pressed Iron Range mining country and turned to drugs after being abused by his father. He also said he wandered around the countryside finding trouble as well as part-time work, and finally became a poker dealer in a bordering Wisconsin casino following a hitch in the service.

When they returned to their hut, Charley kept so close that the cop felt he may have adopted a brother. To avoid utter boredom, he showed his new buddy some card tricks he learned in the Army until some grouch needing sleep soon turned the lights off on them.

Sleep, however, didn't come quickly for Joe due to the new surroundings, the loud snoring, and even the stench from the very dirty hut and unwashed humans occupying it. But he finally dozed off despite all this and was sound asleep when suddenly awakened by a noise that seemed to be from under his bed—where Joe had placed his radio and wallet.

Instantly, Joe grabbed his flashlight from under his pillow and focused it down on some guy caught reaching for his radio. At the moment the light flashed, the burly night thief jumped up and took a swing at Joe. His fist missed, but it was so close and powerful that the cop could feel a gust of air from the force of the hefty swing. Quickly rolling out the other side of the bed, Kavinsky faced his attacker, with flashlight in hand. The thief swung again, this time knocking the flashlight on the floor. The light went out and Joe thought he'd also be out if that giant fist struck him.

The cop kicked his foot karate style into the groin of the scowling man, doubling him up for the moment. He also threw a lucky hard punch in the dark that contacted the guy's chin, knocking him against the wall near the bed. This only made the attacker more furious. He drew a long blade from his belt and lunged for Joe standing near a window. The fighting cast an eerie reflection through the window as the bed light flickered. Some passersby outside silently watched this violent struggle.

But, surprisingly, the action stopped abruptly. Nothing happened. As though on command, Charley Johnson came out of nowhere and delivered a blow on the would-be thief's head with a chair that left the attacker staggered and then unconscious at the foot of the bed.

Joe wasn't sure it was charley until the lights came on and someone, interrupted by the noise of the conflict, bellowed: "Hey, hombres, what the hell's going on? Knock it off!"

The commotion caused security to come running and they hauled the attacker off screaming. The following morning Joe again said his thanks to Charley, his very faithful companion and they celebrated together with a breakfast of stale toast and what could possibly be large lizard eggs,

"God, this is awful. It's a crime!" grumbled Charley. "This whole place stinks." Joe agreed. After forcing down some more swill, or whatever it was they were eating, they then set out for work in the compound located near the Beck manor and the nearby beach. The walk down the unpaved road was especially tough on Joe's foot in the shoe with the gun, but he was very careful to walk normally knowing that both he and Charley were probably being closely watched by passing security guards.

CHAPTER 16

Robert Beck's spacious office in his English Tudor style home, which sat on the town's tallest hill in a kingly fashion overlooking the Atlantic Ocean, allowed him a very impressive panoramic view of the beach on which the cop was approaching.

Beck paid no attention to Kavinsky's overcrowded Jeep since this was often the route that his workers took to get to the beach near the airport hangars. Besides, he had much on his mind that morning. This was the day he was to depart for Bogota to talk to some of his cartel associates. For Beck, traveling was a very serious business and could take him almost anywhere in the world—except to the United States where he was still wanted by the feds for his alleged role in narcotic trafficking and embezzlement.

Beck notified his secretary of his schedule and, escorted by two large blacks, left in one of the stretch limousines parked in front of his mansion for his private restaurant at the airport. The vehicle in which Joe was riding, in fact, was only a few minutes away from crossing the path of his limo as it neared the beach.

As usual, Beck spent much of his time in the privacy of his big automobile making phone calls. Once in the restaurant, he was one of only several men in suits sitting around a table, with the others posted at the doors. The sixtyish-looking vice lord appeared cocky, arrogant and secure with every movement of his body. There was no sign of the humble boy he used to be, who grew up in the Midwest and attended convent schools. You could tell at a glance that he was a bottom-line, no-nonsense guy despite his gentlemanly mannerisms and tone of voice. Those who met him said his eyes were green and cold and seemed to study your very soul when they looked at you. With Beck, there was no faking it. If he found out you were lying to him or weren't up front with him in any way you were history.

The drug leader was being briefed this morning on the purpose of his cartel visit. Many of the drug kingpins around Bogota were still in power and numerous banks still laundered drug money, and lots of it. What couldn't be laundered in Colombia could be in even isolated islands where bankers welcomed money of any kind. Beck seemed driven by money, which explains why he was attracted to the banks of the Bahamas. He left his home, wife and family in the states many years ago. And he was still being attracted by it virtually everywhere underworld money was apt to accumulate.

Beck continued to ignore Joe's Jeep even when it went directly by the front window of the restaurant on the way to Hangar No. 5, where new workers were oriented before going to work. He knew that his heavily armed organizational structure would not permit anyone to be on his grounds without proper clearance and that newcomers would not only be thoroughly checked but also closely observed at all times. Rigid penalties were enforced by his expanding security system. Some

violators, Joe was told, were never heard of again. His procedure dictated that anyone in question should be escorted by a so-called companion well indoctrinated in the ways of Mr. Beck. The companion was usually a big enforcer carrying a semi-automatic. Anyone considered suspicious seemed doomed from the start.

By the time Beck and his escorts finished their breakfast discussion, Joe and Charley already were assigned to cleaning out a storage room of equipment parts stored in Hangar 6. While mechanics scurried about working on the planes, mostly four or six-place twin engine craft, the cop and his buddy were counting parts and placing them neatly in cartons to be moved to another hangar.

During this time, Joe's eyes wandered around to spot anything special. It wasn't until he began moving the cartons, however, that he noticed some detailed flight information posted on a dirty wall. Stopping to light a cigarette, he glanced at the schedules and noticed that one of the planes being checked out in this hangar was destined for none other than Minneapolis. However, before he could find when the Twin Cities flight was to depart Charley came by to borrow a smoke.

Joe was prepared for this. He immediately drew out a special pack of cigarettes that he obtained in Nassau and flicked one into Charley's waiting fingers He knew these were loaded with lots of marijuana, called "Mary Jane" by his associates, and that his friend would get the high he wanted after only a few drags.

"How do you like this place so far?" questioned the cop's companion who blew out a big puff of smoke. It was obvious to Joe that Charley was apparently trying to take him into his confidence again.

"I'll go bonkers if this is all we're going to do. I thought we'd be into some big-time operations and that we'd be bringing in loads of money by now," responded Joe with a scowl. "This is boredom plus. But don't worry kid, I have a feeling that things will liven up soon."

"What makes you think that?"asked Charley.

"Once we get paid, man. We'll make this old town rock."

"Right, man," the young man responded with a grin as though Joe's reply was the one he wanted to hear. He gave his cigarette another puff, coughed, and then remarked, "Man, Joe, this joint is the greatest. I'm already rocking high."

Kavinsky could see Charley was starting to be off by himself After another drag, in fact, his companion sort of drifted away from him When he was gone far enough, Joe again glanced at the flight notices. He was right, there was a flight to Minneapolis, via Miami. It was due out in two days, at 4;30 p.m. and loaded, Joe was sure, with drugs.

While continuing to move parts, the cop also obtained a good overview of the grounds outside. Several other hangars were around the one he was in and also were filled with workers and maintenance crews as well as many airplanes. It wasn't until he boarded the Jeep again and headed to one of the other hangars that he noticed what apparently was Beck's classy jet.

It glistened in the hot sun and obviously was a very expensive sea plane. You could tell it was well maintained and frequently polished. Like a good horse it was manicured and ready to win the sweepsteaks, thought Joe. Only the rider, Beck, held the bridle. But many could hop on. It was capable of flying at least 20 or more passengers. One of the English speaking Cubans told him recently that the interior of the jet alone cost nearly $10 million.

Joe also caught sight of the elegantly dressed drug lord as Beck and his bodyguards walked rapidly toward the fancy plane.

Kavinsky turned the Jeep sharply to get to the next work hangar, allowing him to get an even closer look at the "king" and his armed entourage. Beck seemed rather small next to them but very erect to maintain his boss-like image. A cigarette hung from his lips as he talked quickly to one of the men placing his luggage into the aircraft. The plane was only half inside the hangar. The fuselage housing the luggage and tail could still be seen outside as the two-man pilot crew prepared for take-off.

Joe turned his head away when Beck looked his way. He was certain the cartel boss wouldn't be able to identify him, but he wasn't taking any chances. Who knows where a cop's picture might be posted for druggies and the mob could see, he thought. With Beck's link to the drug network around the Caribbean and South America he realized if he was caught his fate could be as bad or worse than the one that befell DEA agent Kiki Camarena, who was tortured and blown away in Guadalajara.

The cop could almost feel the tiny pistol under his feet as he got closer to the notorious drug dealer. He realized he should switch this weapon as soon as possible on returning to the hut so it would be in a more readily accessible place. Since he was already on the dealer's turf, he thought it best to simply put the gun under his belt, hidden by his over-sized, garrish-looking shirt covering the weapon.

The Jeep stopped at the hangar next to Beck's aircraft which was now revving up for the flight to Colombia. Within moments, Joe was moving parts around again with his fellow workers. After moving only two boxes, he heard Beck's plane take off. It was a smooth departure, with the jets leaving a brilliant stream through the blue skies in the direction of Colombia.

Joe and his work crew were hungry that evening and none of the bulky food on the tables was left as they made their way back to their sleeping quarters. Charley was with him again, asking for another joint and wondering if he had coke to spare. Joe said he was frisked for the stuff and had to leave it behind when he left the states. Charley still hung around, however, and it wasn't until the camp boss yelled lights out again that Joe had any chance to make his gun switch.

The next day, Kavinsky didn't spot Charley until about noon, when he came on him with some workers who were sniffing some white stuff. He thought it strange that the young man was not joining in with the others.

"Working on parts again?" asked the cop, wondering if he'd be with this guy once more in the heat of the afternoon.

"Naw man…I'm history. I'm heading back to the mainland. I don't dig all this grunt work."

This took Joe by surprise. As they proceeded toward the mess hall, he probed further.

"I guess it ain't so easy to break away from here…are you sure you can do it Charley?"

"No sweat man. I have my plans, do you have yours?"

"What do you mean plans? How the hell could I have any plans.there's no place for me to go," Joe said shrugging his shoulders.

"You ought ta catch a ride back home on the Minnesota airplane tomorrow, man," Charley replied, looking straight at Joe with a slight smile. "Hell, it's going right to Minneapolis."

"You're shitting me!"

"No I'm not. I've helped to load stuff on that plane many times. The pilot boards at 4:25 and we have to get it completely loaded by 3:30."

He added, "Hell, it leaves right from around that hangar you and I worked in the other day."

"Hangar 6?"

"Yeah, that's the one. It's a twin-engine Beech plane. Those damn things I understand bounce all around up there—but it gets ya where you want to go."

"Any chance I can get a good look at it taking off?" Joe asked casually as though he simply wanted something to do.

"Sure, try to get to hangar 6 on time and I'll bet you can even help load up," said Charley as he spotted a place to sit down and grabbed some potatoes passing by on a plate.

"What's there to load?" asked Joe, hoping he wasn't pressing his companion too much to arouse any suspicion.

"I told you, man…stuff. Enough to blow lots of noses around Minnesota," Charley said with a grin.

Joe backed off. And after eating another disgusting meal, and pouring down some horrible shit-colored solution called coffee, he left for his bunk to put on some clean socks. The ones he had on were the same he wore in the Bahamas and their foot odor was beginning to nauseate even Kavinsky. While looking for a clean pair, he noticed that his clothes appeared to hang differently than the way he hung them up the night before. Upon closer inspection, he was sure that someone had been going through his belongings. Everything was back on the hangars, but not the way he would have left it.

Thinking that someone might be on to him, Kavinsky definitely decided to get the hell off Bimini as soon as possible. He knew he didn't stand a chance to escape if he had to go through that phony customs again and that someone would report his departure before he could even get a mile down the road.

The more he thought, the more he became convinced that the only chance to save his ass was to catch that flight at hangar 6 He wondered if his buddy Charley knew how helpful he had been with his information. Charley was still a mystery to the cop who figured him as just another informer for Beck and couldn't be trusted. Then again, Joe realized Charley also could be setting him up.

For the rest of the afternoon, the cop worked outside in torrid temperatures, pulling weeds from around walks leading to some of the offices near the airstrip. A few of his projects offered a good view of hangar 6 and helped him map out some strategy for getting to the Minnesota-bound plane. Apparently Charley was intent on skipping, he didn't show up even at the mess hall that evening

In fact, it wasn't until lunch time the next day that he saw his companion again. Charley nudged between Joe and a fat Mexican as the cop reached for some water on the table.

"You all set to travel mister Kav...er...Barrott?" he asked almost in a whisper.

"Huh—what travel?" asked Joe nearly forgetting to respond to his alias. He was too occupied with thoughts of Sarah to ask what's going on. But he wondered why Charley was having trouble with his name. It almost sounded as though he was about to say Kavinsky.

"I'll be on your Jeep to the hangar," whispered back Charley, who was obviously uncomfortable being so close to the angry looking dude next to him.

"I gotta go now...stay close, keep your eyes open, and look for me," Charley said.With that, Charley rose from his chair and quickly departed.

Joe remained somewhat puzzled by all of this even after the ride to the hangar. When they arrived and started moving parts again, the cop could already see the Minnesota plane on the strip. He also spotted Charley, wearing a sombrero, moving toward a truck loaded with containers. He began walking toward the truck as Charley's eyes met his and seemed to beckon him ahead.

Joe leaped on the truck just as it started out toward the plane. He and Charley were the only passengers besides the driver and Joe felt too exposed during the bumpy ride that took them in an area where they could be easily picked off by a sniper.

As soon as the truck stopped, Charley hopped off and began handing the containers to the loading crew. He motioned Joe to do likewise, but before he could grab any of the containers one of the crew made a dash toward him and collapsed, hitting the cement pavement as a gun shot cracked.

Almost instinctively, the cop reached for his pistol but wondered who to aim it at. The crewman lay dead almost at his feet, with a hole in his bleeding head. Joe finally pointed the gun at Charley who pushed it aside as he made a run toward the door of the plane.

"Don't Kavinsky—I'm your friend. I'm DEA!"

Confused, especially by Charley knowing his real name, Joe lowered the gun and commanded, "prove it pal!"

"Don't ask questions…just get in the plane," urged Charley, flashing a Drug Enforcement Administration ID badge. Charley also drew out a pistol and pushed it against the head of the pilot waiting to take off.

"Move over amigo, or you are one dead hombre!" Charley warned the Cuban pilot.

The pilot obeyed promptly. It was then that Joe spotted movement in the area where the shot seemed to come from that killed the crewman. He whirled around and saw a large heavily-bearded man with a shotgun running toward him with rage in his eyes.

"Shoot him, Kavinsky! Kill him before he kills you!" shouted Charley. "He meant to kill you but shot the co-pilot instead."

Joe turned toward the running feet and fired straight on, hoping that the attacker with the gun was near enough for his little pistol to pick him off.

The shotgun went flying from the big guy's hands as he hit the pavement on his face only a few feet from the plane. Joe could see blood oozing from his attacker's chest as both he and Charley crowded into the cockpit with the bewildered pilot.

"Now man—now—take it up! Fly this crate or I'll blow your fuckin head off!" ordered Charley poking his .38 at the pilot's head. Upon closing the cockpit window, Joe could still hear shooting all around the area and realized Beck's men were closing in fast. To help get the plane going he also pushed his gun into the pilot's belly. "Si si" were the only words uttered by the nervous guy at the controls as he pulled out the throttle making the plane head toward the takeoff strip.

"Faster you bastard—open it up. Pronto! Pronto!" growled Charley. But despite all this pushy encouragement, however, Joe thought he heard a bullet nick a wing as the small craft rolled down the runway.

"Darse prisa!" commanded his DEA buddy, urging the pilot to hurry up in Spanish. "No funny stuff. I'm also a pilot and I'll shoot your damn brains out if you slow down." Joe looked back at the hangars and could see his pursuers still chasing the plane, skirting the two bodies lying where they were hit. He was also hoping that Charley wasn't bull-shitting when he said he knew how to fly.

"Up! Up!" ordered the DEA agent as he pressed his pistol harder against the pilot's skull. As if to obey, the plane instantly began nosing into the sky as Joe's fingernails dug nervously into his fist—as though trying to help the pilot reach the clouds and get the hell out of harm's way. As the ocean came into view, Kavinsky's tension lessened, realizing that they were at last out of range of high-powered guns. He caught sight of a ship a few miles from shore and knew it wouldn't be long before they were over land again—this time in Miami.

"Move this bastard to the back!" demanded Charley. "I'll take over the controls, and keep your gun on him until we land. He's part of the cartel group and can't be trusted."

Joe pushed the narcotics runner to a back seat and sat next to him. Gaining confidence in the flying skills of Charley, Joe then leaned forward to converse with Charley.

"Tell me friend, how the hell did you know my name and could trust me?"

"Don't worry, we have our ways…even though the press might emphasize our failures and not our many successes," Charley said with a smile.

Joe wasn't to be put off "There was no way you could have known. I didn't tell anyone."

"The DEA has lots of ears, Joe. We even think your Judge Sims had connections with the Afghans in dealing with drugs and opium. Some flights were loaded with payments from the Twin cities in return for illegal drugs He had some good contacts—like he did with Pelot."

"But the only person that knew my whereabouts was Sarah."

"And Sarah has an identical twin sister. Right Joe?" Charley was almost leading Kavinsky on like a parent does with a child. Silence prevailed The cop was trying to figure out what the DEA agent was trying to say.

"Are you telling me Susan Crimmons had something to do with all this?"

"Somewhat—only indirectly. We have many connections, Joe, sometimes with the strangest people."

"I get it. Sarah told Susan and Susan got to your guys," Joe said snapping his fingers.

"Umm—not exactly. Susan may not be our side," said Charley. "Don't assume anything," he cautioned turning his head to look Joe in the eyes. "How do you know your thief that night wasn't looking for those bank serial numbers? How do you know he really wasn't out to do a hit on you?" He added, "Someone must have thought you had those numbers...someone you know very well perhaps."

Looking sternly at the DEA pilot Joe asked, "Your name isn't Charley is it? It's got to be an alias—you guys operate like us in a way." He then added, "And what do you know about Susan?"

"Terry Johnson's the name. Hell—I'm probably more Scandinavian than most of you norsky lads in Minnehoota ya betcha, at least lots more than a Kavinsky" the agent teased. "My Spanish and suntan help me look Cuban at times. Hell, I'm such a good match, my boss gave me the Bimini assignment to watch over you. I've kept a good eye on your Bahama whereabouts."

"And...? "continued Joe waiting for an answer to his question about Susan.

"And what?" responded Johnson

"And how the hell do you know Susan and where does she fit in?"

The amateur pilot put his earphones back on while peering more intensely, obviously ignoring Joe's inquisition. After some hesitation he continued, "I think you may have Sarah and Susan mixed up Joe—easy to do when they look so much alike, right? One of them isn't involved at all with where the crack's going on this airplane ride, but the other one...well, maybe a little."

"And who is it?" Joe asked, his eyes narrowing and fearful of the response.

"Relax—Sarah is clean,but just about everyone else who is anyone in your area isn't."

"Such as?"—Joe asked again,not to be denied an answer.

"Such as some of your bank presidents, corporation heads, doctors,.lawyers, maybe even indian chiefs and many others with influence." He added, "Hell—even judge Sims was watching every drug flight that came and went. He knew the schedules, but he knew too much and they did him in.

"Hell, Joe, some of your bankers and judges up there even have their own hit men to protect their drug interests."

"How do you know that? Not even the cops know that much for sure."

"Exactly…but more cops than you expect are in on it. As to how I know, let's say we have our informants. People that are willing to stick their necks out to what they suspect, what they see and hear."

"And that's where Susan fits in…right?" concluded Joe.

"Wrong—although mother and daughters knew a lot about what was happening. Susan was, much closer to her dad. She worked with him and tattled on you and your uncle to the mob."

"But you're a junkie yourself. You were dragging on that joint I gave you."

"I was faking it man. Like Bill Clinton—I didn't inhale", laughed Johnson. "But I did get a mighty whiff of it…that's when I left to cough in private. You sure had that last one loaded."

Before Joe could ask any more questions, the plane ride became bumpy and then lurched suddenly as Charley turned very serious and pointed a finger to the sky at the right of the aircraft. "My God, they've sent up a pursuit plane to get us," Johnson warned.

Kavinsky spotted a jet approaching that was bearing the same markings as Beck's fleet in the Bimini hangars.

"It'll shoot us down if we can't get through to the Miami Coast Guard," exclaimed Johnson almost yelling as he tried turning the omni radio to pick up the Florida coast. He hollered out :"May Day!…May Day! This is DEA Johnson in his Big Bob Beechcraft 4589 seaplane. Bearings: North/Northwest heading toward coast, 20 miles off Key West. Being pursued for destruction by Cuban Lear jet marked Big Bob, 3290. Now maneuvering to stay clear Need help immediately to fight off jet. Please hurry."

Joe quickly brought his gun out again and pressed it against the Cuban's head. "You son of a bitch, if we do go down you'll be the first to feed the fish."

"Senior, senior—let me land," the Cuban pleaded. I know how to set this down. Otherwise we'll all be blown apart."

"He's right, Kavinsky. I'm not much good at landing on choppy waters with pontoons," Johnson shrugged as he made room for his replacement. Joe could see the jet rapidly coming closer, leaving a silvery vapor trail in the partly cloudy sky. Johnson turned as if trying to find something.

"This crate should have a shotgun or two, but where do they hide them?" Johnson asked Joe in desperation.

"You—Pedro—are there any guns in this plane?" Kavinsky asked the Cuban pressing the nozzle of his gun a bit further into the side of his head.

"Si—behind the back seats. There should be two Uzys and an AK-47."

Joe looked around quickly, groping in a frantic attempt to feel anything resembling a gun within reach. Frustrated, he crawled to the back on his knees around the other seats searching for any type of firearms.

"Aha!—here they are…they're Uzys and an AK alright. These guys really come well prepared." He checked them over, making sure they were loaded and passed one to the agent.

"Hell, we won't have a prayer against their rockets Joe," warned Johnson. "Our only hope is the Coast Guard."

With that, their craft shook and lurched suddenly to the left.

"Our tail was nicked badly on takeoff. Or they may have fired something off already from that jet," explained Johnson. "We're like sitting ducks."

"They're telling us to land, seniors. Unless we do we will all die," warned the frightened Cuban pilot.

"Perhaps. But they certainly don't want to destroy this plane. It's got too much stuff in it…it's much too valuable to be sunk," noted Johnson.

"So what do we do?" asked Joe. "Descend to the water?"

"We have no other choice, although if we stay around this area we may be picked up by the Coast Guard but the druggies can still get to us," Johnson pointed out.

"You mean they'll try to come aboard?"

"You're damn right. And the only things that will get dumped overboard are you and me," predicted the DEA agent.

With that, another warning shot shook their plane.

"Okay poncho...I've heard enough. Nose her down!" commanded Kavinsky, resigned to their perilous, watery fate. Both Joe and Terry began looking in the plane for anything resembling an inflatable raft or life-preservers at this point but they could only come up with what looked like special pillows that, hopefully, may give them floating time in the choppy water waiting to swallow them.

CHAPTER 17

As their craft began its descent, Johnson again notified the U.S.Coast Guard of their approximate location and pending disaster. "DEA Johnson, DEA Johnson…Beechcraft going down under fire from Lear jet with red markings…about 18 miles off coast from Bimini. Need fire-power to avoid blow up Please hurry…will be on water soon."

"What's our exact fix? Give me our fix or I'll blast your head off now!" Kavinsky ordered the pilot. "No comprendo!…no comprendo!" answered the frightened Cuban as sweat streamed down his face.

"Forget it Joe. He knows the coordinates and how to read them on this plane but he also knows he'll be safer to let his guys come and get him."

As the water came closer, the lapping waves appeared bigger—just waiting to cover them up. No doubt about it, landing would be terribly risky. "Great—we'll either drown or be shot," commented Kavinsky.

The Beck jet was now so close its numbers could be clearly seen. What's more, the several rockets under its wings also were now very noticeable.

"We're going in gents. Get ready to sink and shoot it out!" cautioned Johnson.

"I don't suppose you have any flack jackets?" asked Kavinsky almost jokingly.

"Nope—but they may need some if we hit a few of them in our cross fire," responded Johnson.

They were now only seconds away from touch down. Johnson gave a last look around as he tightly grasped his Uzy.

"God—I don't believe it!"

"What's up?" asked Joe getting ready for the landing shock, as he nervously blessed himself with the sign of the cross and hoped to God for survival.

"Isn't that a couple of jet fighters?"

Joe had to squint to look out the misty window. What seemed to be two small shiny objects on the horizon began to sprout wings and were swiftly approaching ahead of bright vapor trails.

"Suppose they're ours?" questioned Joe hopefully.

"Must be—they're coming from our side," noted the agent.

"Don't land—take her up!" shouted Joe. "You heard him take it up!" Johnson pressed his Uzy into the pilot's big belly to reinforce this command.

With two or three more thrusts of the Uzy, the pilot began nosing the small plane once again toward the sky.

The Lear was now to their right. It had to circle and come back to destroy them. But by the time it would once again get its sights on the Beechcraft the U.S. fighters should be in range.

"Look—by god they're flying away! they're going on! They're not coming back. Our guys have scared them off," shouted Kavinsky.

Johnson's radio began squawking. "DEA…DEA…Coast Guard spots you. Lear in sights. Situation back to normal. Proceed to destination. Police on hand!"

"Hallelula!…we're home free!" yelled Joe.

"I'll take over now amigo," Johnson told the Cuban. "I'm sure I can float this in at the Ft. Lauderdale harbor."

"Why Lauderdale? Why not Miami International?" questioned Joe.

"That's our agency's check-in point," explained the DEA agent. "This plane wasn't planning to land there…it was going directly up to one of your 10,000 Minnesota lakes. But that's before you and I took over"

"Which lake?"

"Ask our friend here." Johnson motioned to the Cuban who was now settled in the co-pilot's seat and could only mumble once more, "No comprendo!"

"I'm sure it was White Bear Lake. Do you have one called that?" asked the agent.

"Yep, very close to the cities," said Joe rather proudly.

"You've got a bad problem up in your cities friend," continued Johnson. "There's two factions of cocaine dealers…and they're feuding against one another." He added, "I'll bet they're blowing one another away already to see who gets this great load of drugs."

"Is it worth a lot?"inquired Kavinsky.

"Probably the biggest drug haul in years. I'm sure it's the most valuable ever in the Twin Cities area. Must be worth a billion dollars. I had inside information working undercover on the Bimini project. It includes every drug imaginable to mankind and womankind, including heroin, methamphetamine, crack cocaine, and even those rape party drugs called ecstasy and GBL Some of the wild things they're pushing now, Joe, you hardly know you're using them until they kill you."

"No wonder they didn't want to sink this aircraft," Joe exclaimed wiping his brow. "What happens next?"

"We'll probably count the stuff once we put the pilot here behind bars. We'll have to keep those guys waiting for it up north. Sure would like to be there to greet them, though. You know—surprise! surprise!. I'm sure they're already upset they didn't rake in that last big haul from the islands. Don't know who got the payout. But I should have more answers when I get to Lauderdale."

He added, "Do you know who's suppose to get all this?"

"Our pilot probably knows better than me—but I guess he isn't speaking to us anymore," Johnson said grinning at the Cuban.

"Any ideas at all Terry?" probed Joe.

"Yeah, somewhat. I heard there's probably some guy named Sapel and several big shots at your banks. I also understand there may be some teachers from your law schools who are regular customers of the Bimini run, along with some corporate executives. There's another guy, too, I can't remember." He continued with a smile. "But I guess they're mostly part of your so-called Irish Mafia."

"You going to arrest them?"

"Are you kidding. You never get the real big honchos. We'll probably just snag one or two of the errand boys and maybe even let them go with the pressure we get from their influential bosses.

"It's awfully damn discouraging, Joe. You get these guys so close to the slammer and you can't put them in because of the big shots profiting from all this trafficking. There's so many making money from these flights that it's tough to blow the whistle on anyone."

Terry looked at Kavinsky, "You know what I mean? I'm sure you run into this up there. If you pursue some of those heavy hitters you could lose your job...and maybe even your life. You're being watched all the time if you suspect the guys in control and they suspect you That's why I was told to keep an eye on you in Bimini. The power boys were catching on to you. You were just about duck soup before we blew that place."

"Yeah—I know," shrugged Joe, wondering how the hell Terry got so street smart so young. Joe was also thinking how to get home fast. "Is there a commercial flight to Minneapolis from Lauderdale?" he asked.

"Suppose so, but I can help get you on a DEA plane. However, it could be a very tight squeeze considering this haul and our interest in sending our guys up there to check things out."

"Thanks. There are some calls I have to make, though, before I take off again."

After finally landing at Lauderdale amid a great sigh of relief from all aboard, Kavinsky, anxious to board the DEA plane, quickly helped to unload the cache and assisted with getting the pilot safely secured. He then hugged Johnson, thanking him for his help. "I sure owe you pal.

Let me know if I can ever pay you back." Terry gave him his phone number and e-mail address just in case he "ever needed it" and Joe then quickly headed for the nearest phone to call Sarah and his uncle Al.

No one answered at Sarah's place, not even Susan who Joe figured was too busy snooping around for Frank. After a few more tries he hung up, wondering why the sisters didn't get an answering machine installed like he suggested. But on second thought, he realized it may be safer without one—considering their risky situation. Who knows who may have their phones tapped.

Fumbling in his pockets and looking at his watch to make sure he didn't miss the flight home, Joe finally found change for calling his uncle while cussing inwardly for not having a cell phone. However, when the call went through, his aunt Kay was the one to answer. "It's me, Joey—aunt Kay-I'm back from my trip, finally-I have to speak to uncle Al it's very important."

Instead of his aunt's usual quick and cheerful chatter, he was surprised at the silence at the other end of the line. "Aunt Kay, are you there?" He finally heard a weak voice say, "Oh Joe, something dreadful has happened. It's hard to explain. Please come home quickly. I'm afraid your uncle is dying."

CHAPTER 18

Al Benjamin was dying at home. His distraught and ever faithful wife Kay was almost constantly at his bedside. Much of her anxiety stemmed from the doctor's admitted ignorance of what Al was actually dying from. Numerous tests were taken, but none led to any indication of the mysterious ailment killing the reporter.

Kay kept her rosary beads handy as she went about her housework, looking in the dying man's room frequently—as though searching for some sign of hope, or need for further despair. She had planned to transport her now very fragile husband to the Mayo Clinic 75 miles away in Rochester, but the doctors warned her that the trip alone might be his undoing.

The only light in her otherwise dark, gloomy day was her nephew's phone call. She tried to tell Al that Joey was on his way, but she could get no acknowledgement from him between his loud gasps. It was as though his entire breathing was becoming paralyzed. His bronchial difficulties were an initial symptom of his strange illness, she recalled

She first worried about his heart when he came home about a month ago complaining of being short of breath after walking briefly around the block for exercise. Following this, what appeared to be the flu attacked him further weakening his condition and even preventing him from going to work. Finally, a few weeks ago, Benjamin suffered a seizure at home that nearly killed him outright. His muscles went into a

spasm and his breathing even stopped for a few seconds while the paramedics administered CPR. Fortunately, Kay was in his room when the
seizure happened and called the 911 emergency number just in time.

Kay was especially busy following Joe's phone call. As always, she
wanted to have the house as tidy as possible for visitors. In her customary way, she put everything in its place in all the rooms of the modest
four-bedroom house where her family grew up.

It was while she was in the downstairs bathroom, which Al called his
"reading room," when she came upon an unusual-looking bottle of
pills, almost hidden behind her husband's razor blades, shaving cream
and assortment of old combs and toothbrushes Kay often had to caution Al not to keep old medicine around, but despite this he absent-
mindedly put aside many of his outdated pill bottles in the medicine
chest after bouts with routine colds and occasional heart-burn.

With housewife instinct, she began throwing away some of the old
paraphernalia from the chest. But today for some unknown reason, she
looked at the little bottle that stood out from the other pills. Perhaps it
was because the bottle looked somewhat new and still contained fresh
capsules. The label on the bottle simply stated that it was for nerve and
muscle pain and should be taken three times each day.

But Kay noticed that although the label looked official, there was no
name of a doctor or pharmacy on it authorizing use of the pills or any
caution notices. However, there was a date. This also surprised Kay.
Apparently it was only less than a month ago when Al obtained this special medicine. It wasn't like him not to mention to her if he was picking
up some new pills or even seeing a doctor. She smiled, knowing that as
guarded as he thought he was about confiding in her, he was like a child
when it came to telling her about his little aches and pains. But why
wouldn't he talk about this?

While all this was happening, Joe was enroute home on a special
DEA jet, being briefed on what was being snuffed, smoked and injected
these days by a growing number of Twin Cities residents. He felt like an

outsider since it seemed like everyone of any importance was really in on the "know" but him. Just about every stuff imaginable was being unloaded in and around the Twin Cities area, even substances Joe hardly every heard of—including a powerful stimulant known as Crank, Speed, and Hawaii Ice, considered more destructive to the mind and body than even Crack.

He was cautioned by the agents aboard not to mention anything about his discovery in Bimini until the DEA had the chance to properly investigate and make a bust. He was hardly surprised when they told him they didn't wish to inform the local authorities since there weren't sure who or how many of the law enforcement groups in the area they could really trust in this matter.

Before the plane landed at the Minneapolis/St. Paul airport, Joe promised the agents aboard to be part of their undercover investigative team and to keep his mouth shut and eyes open about what was going on. In turn, the DEA promised to keep him closely informed about their plans as to when and how they would blow the whistle on all this Twin Cities criminal drug activity.

Joe also was to be their inside man on the police force, and he was assured that they would do nothing to embarrass him or the "good guys" on the force and that their activities would be sanctioned by the federal and state governments.

With this in mind, Kavinsky put a coin in the first public phone he could spot at the airport to let Sarah know he arrived. He began to feel sorry that he was unable to use his handy cell phone—but knew he would have had it confiscated along with his camera if he took it to Bimini. After several futile attempts, he realized that both Sarah's phone and Al's were busy, so he caught a cab and headed out to his uncle's, not knowing for sure if he'd find him dead or alive.

Upon arriving at Al's and rushing up to his bedroom, Joe was still not absolutely sure if his uncle was among the living. "He's been like this for days Joe," explained his aunt, gazing sorrowfully at her husband. She

pointed to all the hoses connected to Al and said some of these were
keeping him alive by infusing nutrients into his blood stream and helping to prevent his chemistry from going out of control.

Joe was an eager listener while aunt Kay recalled the weird and con-
fusing background leading to his uncle's illness. She described the time
she found the little bottle of pills in her husband's medicine chest. And
that's when Joe stopped her by responding "yes, I know—but tell me
more about what was inside the bottle.

"Have you had those pills analyzed yet?"Joe asked.

"No, I just found them. They were hidden behind all his other old
health-care stuff."

"Any idea where he got them?"

"No…only when," aunt Kay said shrugging her shoulders.

"Was it recently—or are they old outdated ones?"

"The date on the label is rather blurred, probably from Al's smeary
fingers, but I believe it says it was only about eight weeks or so ago."

Joe took the bottle and closely examined it. "It doesn't give the name
of the drug maker, nor any idea where they were made," he murmured,
scratching his head. "And, as you pointed out, there's no name of the
prescribing physician.

"You'd better let me have those pills aunt Kay. I'll have our lab boys
try to determine what they are. It's just a long shot, but they may have
something to do with Al's illness."

He continued, "In the meantime try to think where uncle Al may
have been about two months ago and if he was going to the doctor's for
any thing."

"I certainly will, Joey. But you know Al well enough to know he'd be
telling me about any sickness or pains he was having…he was like a
hypochondriac when it comes to that."

Joe chuckled, knowing the close and wholesome relationship
between his uncle and aunt. But he also knew that Al, being a good

newsman, kept many things to himself when it came to his role as an investigative reporter.

Upon returning home, Kavinsky finally reached Sarah on the phone and told her he'd be stopping by shortly. After assuring her that he'd bring her up-to-date on his travels, he asked if Susan was around. Fortunately, Sarah's twin sister was planning on being home all that week—and as far as Sarah knew Susan was no longer going with Meyer. She also said she was to meet Susan later in the day and that Susan missed Frank very much.

After hanging up, Joe was pondering his conversation with Sarah and began recalling some of his discussion with Terry Johnson regarding Susan. He found it hard to agree with Terry that Susan was implicated in any of this. He must talk with her about it—but when and where? His thoughts quickly returned to his uncle, however, knowing that every moment counted to help keep Al alive. He also began thinking of Benjamin's friends—anyone who might be able to shed a little light on where Al got his mysterious pills.

"Joe Thorne—that's who," thought the cop out loud. He often heard his uncle talk about Thorne, the police reporter who Al seemed to trust and respect. Perhaps Al confided in him before taking sick-maybe Thorne knew where Al got the medicine. Kavinsky's mind kept jumping at any hope of helping his uncle.

He dialed Al's phone number at work—hoping Thorne was closeby.

Joe lucked out. Thorne picked up the phone to let callers know Benjamin was out sick. Unfortunately, however, Thorne had no idea where Al may have been or what he was up to. But before hanging up, the police reporter mentioned that perhaps he should check Al's memo book and calendar to see what Al may have been doing about two months ago. The cop was put on hold for what seemed like half-an-hour before Thorne got back to the phone.

"Joey—Al didn't haven much jotted down. However, there's a little item in his note book on his desk. I can barely make it out. Looks like an appointment he made in November—that'd be a few weeks from the time he got sick."

"Yeah, yeah" responded Joe, pushing Thorne to get on with it.

"Your uncle scribbles a lot. But it looks like a doctor's name."

"Can you make it out at all?" asked Kavinsky.

"Hmmm—I believe it says a Dr. Nanty."

Realizing Al's c's often look like t's, Kavinsky asked, "could it be doctor Nancy?"

"Yeah—you know you're right...it could be."

"Any idea of the time of the call?"

"Sure—he's got it written down at 10 a.m."

"On what day?"

"Wednesday, November ninth."

"Why the questions Joe? Are you on to something?" the curious reporter probed.

"Don't know yet...but thanks for the info."

Upon hanging up, the cop quickly checked the phone books for Dr. Klein's office number. Visibly disturbed over this conversation, his fingers shook somewhat as he flicked the numerous pages of physician listings in both the metro and suburban directories.

"That bitch, she may have had something to do with Al's trouble," he spoke to himself. "Damn—why didn't I check this out earlier—but I told Al not to pry into this any further until I got back."

Finally finding the number, he got a busy signal on his first call. But after dialing again he apparently reached the doctor's receptionist. He could feel his heart pumping and heard a rather rude voice inform him that the doctor was unavailable and that she was not expected in until that afternoon. Asked if he wished to make an appointment, Kavinsky was caught somewhat off guard and searched for an appropriate reason for his call. The one he came up with even made him surprised.

"Yeah—I'm Al Benjamin. The doctor put me on pills the other month and the label fell off. I know I was only supposed to be on them for a short time. I'm wondering if you could tell me when I was in last so I don't exceed my dosage?"

There was a pause at the other end. Joe felt the receptionist he was talking to might be suspicious. He was greatly relieved when the she finally replied after a few moments—"Yes, Mr. Benjamin—our records show you were in on November ninth to see Dr. Klein. However, you'd have to check with her regarding your dosage. I'll be sure to tell her you called and may be calling back."

Joe nearly bit his lip. "No, you don't have to bother her. I have pills left and I know she wanted me to continue taking them for a couple of months." Fortunately, the receptionist didn't wish to inquire further and simply said, "Well, if you want to call her she'll be at the office after 3.p.m."

The cop knew immediately he may have blown it. If the receptionist told her Benjamin called she might know that by now Al should be too sick—or even dead—to contact her. It was very important that he pay a call on Klein before the receptionist can inform her about his inquiry. He had to get to the doctor's office before she arrives.

However, he still had several hours to stop off at Sarah's—so he headed out to see her and rekindle romantic ties and update her on his uncle. When he arrived, he eagerly made up for lost kisses and hugs with Sarah. It was during their long embrace that he thought he spotted Susan stepping out from the shadows near a corner bedroom. She seemed to be grinning in the background.

This distracted Joe somewhat, making him recall what Johnson said about Susan. It was as though he saw Susan in an entirely different light, now that he knew she may also be dealing with the drug traffickers.

It interrupted him so much that he nodded to Susan and said, "We need to talk—you're living very dangerously you know."

"I don't know what you mean," Susan said. "You seem to be living pretty recklessly yourself with Sarah," she laughed.

"Really Susan, I know what's going on," Joe declared seriously.

"What do you mean Joe?…what exactly do you know?" asked a puzzled Sarah looking at both her lover and twin sister.

"I can't talk now. But trust me. Right now I have to visit a doctor to help my uncle Al."

"You mean there's still some hope?" Sarah questioned.

"I'm hoping to find that out from the doctor."

When Joe entered the waiting room of Dr. Klein, there was no one there to greet him. The receptionist must have left for a break, he thought. It was also strange, however, that there were also no patients anywhere. This created a rather eerie feeling as he sat down on one of the many empty chairs in the rather large unoccupied waiting area.

When the receptionist did show up, he was somewhat startled. Her voice wasn't pleasant—loud and rough. A smoker, Joe figured, and perhaps maybe a boozer Someone you wouldn't expect on the staff in a doctor's environment.She didn't fit the image.

"Are you Benjamin?" she asked between coughs. As the cop nodded, the phone rang and she lowered her voice for a few minutes as though whispering to the person at the other end. Upon hanging, up, she announced once more in a coarse voice, "Dr. Klein won't be in today. Something came up unexpectedly—Sorry."

"When can I see her?"

"She should be in tomorrow morning. But call before you come."

He knew something was wrong. This woman was definitely a phony. He got up as though to leave, but instead approached her desk at the check-in counter. Without saying another word, he showed his badge and stared at the startled woman behind the desk.

"Did Dr. Klein just phone you?" With that he grasped the arm of the woman and forced her forward. "Answer me!—I'm detective Kavinsky of the police."

Startled, she almost spilled her coffee while fumbling for words. "Yes, but she, she…has to be at the hospital this afternoon. Some emergency came up." Trying to regain her composure, she asked, "but I thought you were Al Benjamin."

"Did you tell her Benjamin was here?"

"Yes. But she said she didn't know any Benjamin."

"Look lady. This is a police matter. You're not to talk to Klein any further until I've contacted her…understand?" He used his most commanding voice, hoping to intimidate her enough that he could be assured of surprising the doctor.

"If you say anything to her, you will be open to police prosecution. We have your phones tapped. This is a very serious situation. Do you understand?" The now frightened receptionist shook her head yes. "Good—now where can I find Klein?"

"All I know is that she usually comes in after her swim in the mornings—about 9 or so."

Joe knew there was still a risk that the receptionist would get to Klein again before he arrived at the exclusive swimming pool. But he had no choice. He had to get to the doctor to find out if there is any way to save Al, regardless of the consequences. Damn—he didn't even know what Klein looked like. But he knew that his friend the lifeguard would be able to point her out if he was there.

He was also certain, however, that Klein's call to the receptionist was to find out if it was really Al Benjamin waiting for her. If it was, he surmised, the phony receptionist and the doctor would plan to finish his uncle off if Al showed up at the time they suggested.

His only hope now was to go head-on with Klein at the swimming pool. As he was thinking of this, he dialed police headquarters and asked for Charley McKay, his narc friend on the force and perhaps one of the few he could really depend on these days. He asked McKay to get in touch with the doctor's receptionist, question her about Klein, and hold her overnight until he was able to talk directly with the doctor.

McKay hesitated at first not knowing what was up, but knew Joe was dealing with a very serious situation So he drew up a search-and-hold warrant and proceeded carrying out Kavinsky's instructions. There was still no assurance, of course, that the doctor would even be at the pool.

There were also lots of questions and doubts swimming around in Kavinsky's mind.

He was still in doubt when he awoke early the next morning. Packing his gun in his gym case, he headed out to the club not knowing what to expect. He had a hunch that judge Sims felt the same anxiety when he departed for the pool the day he was terminated.

He had a funny feeling in his gut as he approached the swinging doors leading into the pool area. The feeling began while he was in the locker room. For one thing, he was all alone—completely all by himself—apparently all the other swimmers were already in the water or the pool was closed. And yet, according to his watch, he was a few minutes early for lap swim to begin. This feeling increased when he arrived at pool side. There were only several people there—two in the water and one on a bench drying himself off. His young friend Roger the lifeguard wasn't even around the pool area.

At this point, Joe was glad he brought his gym case, knowing his gun was nearby. Not knowing what to do, he put a toe in the water as though testing it before diving in. As usual, it was ice cold The shock of the water, though, felt good. It was like an alarm telling him not to venture in too quickly. Instead, he looked around again and caught the guy on the bench staring back at him.

As though looking for something, Kavinsky sauntered casually over to the bench and smiled at its occupant who glanced away as Joe approached. "Hey—where did our lifeguard go today?" he asked casually.

Not looking up, the man on the bench mumbled something about the guard being sick.

"Gee, that's too bad," said Joe. His next question was more to the point. "Where in the hell is everybody?—this is suppose to be lap swim time."

"Must be their day off. Once in a while we have 'em," mumbled back the fat, bearded bench-sitter.

"Do you know who's in the water?" quizzed the cop.

"No—I'm sort of new here myself."

Realizing he wasn't going to get much information from this guy, Kavinsky gazed at the swimmers trying to identify them if possible. It was tough to see them since they were both excellent lappers, streaking through and slightly under the water like Olympians. Each wore a swim cap and goggles, almost hiding their faces.

When they approached the lane near the bench, however, he could see that one was indeed a female—and a very shapely and graceful one at that.

At this point, the cop jumped into the starting lane. The water seemed to bring him to his senses, making him wonder what in hell he was doing trying to chase after these two "dolphins." He splashed himself with water as though getting the courage to start his laps. Hoping for time, he adjusted his goggles, foggy from the mist, and pulled them over his head. He then could immediately and clearly see that those in the water were circling around to his lane again, at a very rapid clip. He could also see the man on the bench quickly get up and approach the starting lane.

CHAPTER 19

Almost instinctively, Joe submerged and rapidly floated, kicking his feet, to begin swimming. On seeing the closeness of the others he was sorry that he decided to join up with them. But with his head now under water, he could still notice the figure of the mumbler now leering down at the spot he just left, as though searching for him. The cop immediately began stroking as fast as possible. Gazing through the water he knew that even at his fastest he couldn't get out of the way of the swimmer leading the lap soon enough. He also could see that the leader was the woman swimmer—and that most likely she was Nancy Klein.

The arm that suddenly came around his neck did not seem to belong to a woman. It was exceptionally strong, almost lethal as Joe grabbed at it and tried to release the strangle hold it was applying He knew that the next pain he may experience would be a needle prick that would probably leave him paralyzed under this now very turbulent water.

He quit struggling with the arm and instead jabbed his elbow as forcefully as possible into the breast of his attacker. He could hear the scream and felt a slight relief from the arm pressure With that he seized the now limp arm and attempted to turn the woman swimmer around to get the needle from her grasp.

By this time, the other swimmer was also on his back, and both attackers were pulling him down into the bottom of the pool to make certain he became still another drowning victim in the club's now notorious swimming pool.

During this frantic action, Joe could see that the other swimmer was a middle-aged guy resembling Harvey Lawrence. Yes, it was Lawrence. He also could see that both had needles and were bent on thrusting them into his body.

Like a battered child, Joe drew up his legs to ward off any more blows and the threatening poke of the needles. He then kicked his legs with all the strength he had left, throwing both from his body for a moment. This gave him time enough to push up from the bottom and head for the top of the water. Upon rising to the surface, Joe gasped for breath, knowing he would be quickly seized and yanked back under the water by the two expert swimmers determined to kill him.

Unable to yell, he got a glimpse of someone at the other end of the pool wrestling with the guy who was on the bench. It was Charley McKay—he must have followed him to the club. At this point, kavinsky felt strong arms once again grabbing at him and pulling him under. The thrashing about caused McKay to spot kavinsky's peril and he came running to the side of the pool where Joe was being attacked.

The appearance of the narc cop also apparently surprised the attackers, since the male swimmer who was tugging at Joe's legs released his hold and swam off under the water as though dashing to escape. Nancy, however, seemed to become even more obsessed in her desire to kill Kavinsky. It was as if she turned into a screeching demon, scratching Joe's face and arms while searching desperately for the syringe needle she dropped in her rush to stab Joe's anatomy.

Her screaming made it difficult for the struggling Kavinsky to communicate with McKay. He pointed to the other swimmer now climbing up the pool steps to run from the pool area, signaling McKay to seize Lawrence before he escaped. McKay lowered his gun and ran toward the fleeing Lawrence. At this point, Kavinsky aimed his fist at the doctor's open mouth which was now shouting profanities and released a punch that jarred her jaw so violently to one side that he could almost hear it snap. Her body, still jerking emotionally and exhausted in the murder attempt, suddenly went limp.

But before she could sink onto the floor of the 12-foot-deep pool, Joe yanked off her cap and grabbed her hair, dragging her to the corner of the pool. He then pulled her up with him as he climbed the steps back to the surface of the rim of the pool.

Seeing that McKay had captured Lawrence in time, Kavinsky, still somewhat choked and gasping for breath after his ordeal, placed Klein down on the cement surface and ran to help Charley. "That receptionist at the doctor's office—she told me they were ambushing you here, Joe. She wanted no part of it," explained McKay. "I thought I'd be too late, but we didn't know until now that they were planning to finish your uncle off yesterday when they thought he was walking into Klein's office. When they knew it was you—they had to get rid of you here."

Before Kavinsky could respond he heard a shot and saw McKay collapse. Joe at first thought McKay was having a heart attack, but then noticed his shirt was splattered with blood. The shot came from the mumbler who had been sitting on a bench and ended up wrestling with Charley. Joe mistakenly figured the guy was disarmed. The gun probably was concealed under the shooter's towel.

The cop froze, knowing that any move on his part would cause the armed man to fire again. Even Lawrence who was fleeing stopped instantly, in apparent disbelief of what was happening. "Don't be a fool Jerry—they're on to us!" Lawrence cried out, attempting to stop the guy from pulling the trigger again. But the gun stayed pointed straight at Joe's chest, completely ignoring what Lawrence was saying.

A weird Silence filled the pool area as all three men wondered what would happen next while McKay moaned on the floor. It was only when Joe noticed his gym bag nearby that he had any hope for survival. Fortunately Lawrence spoke again, further distracting the armed man.

"Put the gun down, Jerry, damn it. We haven't a chance. If we kill two police officers, every cop around the country will be on our trail."

As the would-be assailant turned to talk to Lawrence, Kavinsky leaped for his bag, grabbed it and rolled over on the floor as he desperately zipped it open and grasped the revolver inside. With both of his attackers surprised and caught off guard, Kavinsky fired his pistol at the upper thigh of the guy with the gun. The bullet made a hole the size of a silver dollar near the mumbler's hip, knocking him backwards screaming with pain. Joe than swiftly moved his gun toward Lawrence, who by now seemed too terrified to move or speak.

"Mac—are you able to get up?" Joe was not only concerned about his partner's well being but also needed all the help he could get to keep this dangerous trio, who were now thwarted in their planned attempt to do away with the nosy cops, from escaping.

The still stunned narcotics detective quickly tore off a section of his shirt and wrapped it around his bleeding arm, applying it like a tourniquet.

"Yeah—I guess," responded McKay weakly. "I'm good enough to rough this bunch up." He arose, reached for the beeper on his belt and began alerting his precinct what was happening. "We need some backup, Joe. I'll stay with these two varmints while you get Klein."

Joe was already running to the spot where Nancy Klein at this time was starting to stir. By the time he approached she was already getting back on her feet and about to dive back in the pool. He dashed to stop her, sliding on the slippery pool floor, and almost caught her ankle before she hit the water again to swim to the far end of the pool where the exit door was located.

In hot pursuit, the cop leaped like a broad jumper as far as he could into the water now swirling around due to the thrashing of bodies. Fortunately, he landed so close to the hysterical Klein he was able to grab her leg. They both submerged and went deep under water as she struggled to swim away.

Being a much better swimmer than Joe, and updated on life-saving techniques, she knew all the right holds to shake loose a supposedly terrified drowning man. Like a marshal arts expert, one of her hands wrapped around his mouth as the other put his arm behind his back.

At this point, the cop was sorry he ever went after Klein on her turf. She took him to the bottom of the pool and put a foot on his head to make certain his lungs would soon be filled with the chlorinated and cloudy pool water. Joe could only make out the figure of the woman above him as he clawed again and again at her leg Before he had to breathe in water, he noticed bright red coming from the deep scratches. Klein could stand it no longer. Wrenched with pain, she suddenly released him and quickly rose to the surface holding her bleeding limb.

Joe also burst from the water gasping. He had no strength left as Klein grabbed the rim of the pool and began hoisting herself up near the door to escape. Whatever McKay yelled, it was commanding enough to stop the doctor in her bloody tracks. Kavinsky could see that Charley was waving his gun and knew he would have fired if she moved any further toward the door.

Kavinsky's anger piqued as he reached the cursing woman and shook her, enraged over what she apparently had done with uncle Al.

"You bitch—tell me what you gave to Benjamin!" To be even more forceful, he began pulling her hair as through intent on tearing it from her scalp.

"Answer me, damn you, or I'll kill you right here and now…my partner won't say anything if I throttle you. You're dead meat, lady, if you don't tell me how to keep my uncle alive." Still squirming and kicking, Klein could only scream louder. "Let me go you bastard, let me go!"

Joe finally flung her down on the floor and appeared to start strangling her, until McKay arrived to hold him back. "Tell me what to give to him…what antedote can we use to counteract that poison you gave him. Do you hear me…I'll wring your pretty neck otherwise."

Klein's expression turned to horror as she realized the cop apparently meant what he was saying.

"Use benzine...benzine," she almost gurgled as his grip tightened around her vocal cords.

"I think she's saying try a medicine called benzine," explained McKay. "Whatever that is."

"What do you mean...witch...what do you mean?" Joe was now shouting directly in her agonized face.

"Tryglycerine Benzine...Tryglycerine Benzine...have it in my office...on shelf in cabinet. Black label on bottle."

With that, the lieutenant loosened his hold. "Mac—take these guys in when the squad comes and get your arm fixed!" Upon getting a reassuring nod from his buddy, Joe ran from the pool, grabbed his pants and, without putting them on over his trunks, burst out of the club and into his police car.

"The brief moments which followed for the cop to reach the doctor's office included breakneck speeds of roaring through several red lights and swerving around traffic jams with his siren on, and almost spinning out of control after nearly missing the entrance to the freeway. But despite all this, he was able to quickly find a convenient parking spot. He ran up to the doctor's office, leaping over every other step of the stairway leading to the doctor's door.

He could tell by the surprised expressions that bursting into the reception area wasn't exactly helping any of the sick people in the waiting room They seemed to turn even more pale at his abrupt and unusual entrance. The nurse in the room could only stare with her mouth open at the strange man in his brief swim-trunks as he wildly tried to find doctor Klein's medical supplies.

After moments of desperation, and flinging some bottles to the floor, he finally discovered the right cabinet door and did a frantic search among the many pills and ointments in all the cabinet drawers.

"Black label…black label," was all Joe could mutter as he peered at every item within his reach. Some of the medicine, however, was out of reach. He noticed a special marked bottle on the tallest shelf, but it was turned around so he couldn't see the label. As the baffled office attendants stood by, Joe found a stool that helped him seize the mysterious container.

Aha!—there it was. A large black label with reverse printing making it difficult to read. It simply stated "For Extreme Poison Emergencies Only! Caution: Use Only As Prescribed for Antidotal Purposes."

"This has to be it!" he exclaimed as the attendants wondered if they should be calling security. He calmed them somewhat upon showing his police badge. Before putting this all in a bag, however, he also spotted a note and tiny knife in a corner of the cabinet. The note had unreadable numbers on it as though faded by water, and the knife seemed to have some blood stains. Nancy must have wrestled it away from the judge, he thought.

Scooping this up, all Joe could mutter to his quizzical audience was: "Thanks…I found what I came after…tell Dr. Nancy to put it on my bill."

CHAPTER 20

At the time the desperate cop was racing back to uncle Al's with the antedote, Susan Crimmons was adding the final touches to her makeup.

She wondered if indeed she could fool the detective even for a minute into thinking she was Sarah, despite what Frank thought. Realizing how similar she was to her sister, she could still tell at a glance the differences. But with just a touch of powder here and a dab of rouge and shadow there, it was remarkable how much closer the similarities became. She whispered to herself a diddy from Disney as she applied her sister's favorite lipstick: "Mirror,mirror on the wall—who's the fairest of them all?…while gazing vainly at her bathroom mirror with a slight smile.

She convinced herself with a smirk that Kavinsky may have been a bit confused as to what twin he was really talking to when she appeared near her bedroom doorway a few hours ago. After all, she reasoned, Sarah was not quite herself and not very communicative since she was virtually talking with a knife to her throat.

Besides, thought Susan enviously, if she had been in Joe's embrace instead of Susan she'd make damn sure he'd still be giving her passionate hugs and kisses. Seems she was always attracted by Joe.

Little did the cop know that both sisters were tipped off about his coming. Both were, in a sense, play-acting, one because she was forced to—the other because she could keep Frank happy and make some big money. It was good that Kavinsky had to leave in a hurry to help his uncle since that made it better for Susan and Meyers. With less conversation, there was less chance that he'd have any inkling as to the whereabouts of Susan's boyfriend, who was being paid by a network of shady contacts who could assure a constant increasing flow of narcotics into the Twin Cities area.

To avoid any interference, both she and Frank had to make sure Sarah was under control. That's why Sarah was now locked in the basement of their home. If necessary, thought Susan, one delay tactic would be to have Joe mistake her for Sarah. She was relying strongly on makeup skills and the perfume Sarah likes so well. After all, many old boy friends got the two of them mixed up, she recalled. Joe may not fall for it, but it was worth the try. The one really bad part of this strange scenario, thought Susan, was that she had to be pushed around so much by Frank and ordered to go along with everything he wanted.

If Kavinsky knew about all this, thought Susan, he would certainly throttle her boy friend.It was as though no one in Susan's circle could do without "Frankie Boy" at this point—at least no one from the Sapel organization, including the police chief and bankers in on the narc runs. Susan was in on this from the start, ever since her father became involved and asked for her help to get on the right side of the mob. She refused at first, but that was before daddy offered her many thousands of dollars to cooperate. He knew Susan was the devious one of the twins. She got into lots of mischief growing up, giving poor Alice considerable grief and problems along the way.

Her mother was reluctant to talk much about her daughters. Sarah was more pacified, more willing to do what her mom would like and less intimidated by her tough-talking and often abusive daddy She was more of a "soul-person," compassionate and wanting the light, right side of life.

Sister Susan was rebellious and took to sniffing cocaine and dating tramps early in life and whenever the mood turned her on. Indeed, it should have been no surprise to anyone who knew her that Susan would pick up with a bum like Meyers. She probably introduced him to her father with a certain pride, pleased that she could bag a dude like Frank as a trophy—the type her shady father would surely admire.

Despite all Susan's faults, however, Sarah would sometimes be easily duped into confiding in her sister. Perhaps it was sort of a big-sister syndrome—since Susan after all was the oldest sister by a matter of minutes. Sarah apparently innocently tipped Susan off about Joe and her plans to go to the Bahamas, despite Joe's warning not to mention this to anyone for fear of danger to both of them and the risk of disclosing his undercover activities.

Although he was sure Sarah would honor his request not to mention anything about this investigation, the thought came to Joe from time to time that sisters—especially twins—might share a secret or two while talking about their men folk The way they giggled together at times like giddy school girls indicated that inwardly they were still very good pals.

By tipping Meyers off about Joe's Bahama trip, Frank could have easily arranged for that thief caught going through Joe's belongings at the Bimini work camp. Also, the DEA could have confused Susan with Sarah as their informer—especially if Susan and Frank tried to manipulate them in any way. Sarah was thinking about all this, too, as Susan completed her makeup. But there was nothing Sarah could do now. She was confined like a prisoner in the basement of the small home where she and Susan resided after their mother's sudden death. She knew Susan would not kill her—but she was sure Frank would find a way to shut her up

Frank was also in the mind of Kavinsky as the waited for word about his uncle at Good Samaritan Hospital in downtown Minneapolis. He couldn't help but feel like wiping out the entire Sapel gang. He sensed that Meyers was the enforcer. But the main reason for thinking about him focused on why Meyers selected Sarah's sister as his girl friend. He suspected it was because she could keep him updated on what the chief investigator of this crime scenario—namely Joe—was up to.

All of this added to the concerns of Joe. But one great burden was removed from his mind when the doctor and aunt Kay came from Al's room to let him know that his uncle would be okay with the antidote and after followup rest and the good care of his beloved wife The cop gave a sigh of relief and made a sign of the cross again in gratitude.

"When can I see him?" asked Joe. "Now, if you want. But make your visit short," cautioned the doctor. "He'll be glad to see you Joey," added his kindly old aunt.

Somewhat absent mindedly, Joe knocked on the door of the hospital room, and then realized his uncle was probably strapped down with tubes, unable to acknowledge his knocking. Upon entering, he knew Al was still in bad shape. He wasn't stirring, but he definitely was still among the living judging from his hard breathing and the noise from the attached cardiac monitor.

Going over to the edge of the bed, the cop looked down and saw his uncle's eyes wide open, looking straight up at Joe.

"How ya doing kid?" asked Al, trying to muster up a smile. Surprised, Joe responded, "God, you sure had me scared, uncle Al."

"How ya doing on that Crimons case?" asked the uncle.

"Hey, unc—time out! You're not suppose to be talking business," Joe warned.

"Aw—I'm okay, thanks to you. That broad doesn't have what it takes to do old Al in," he added with a smile. "But she almost pulled it off."

"You're damn right she almost did. Never underestimate the power of an Olympic female swimmer unc," kavinsky chuckled.

"But we got her all put away. The others I don't know about. But the DEA does, and they're already planning to round them up—including Sapel, the chief and all the rest."

Al started coughing with that bit of news and alarmed Joe when he noticed the heart monitor fluttering somewhat with each cough. "Hey, Al, knock it off will ya…let me do the talking, okay?"

The reporter continued anyway, "What about his henchman Frank Meyers? Get him Joe. Meyers is a blood sucker—and awfully good with a gun or needle. Anything Sapel wants he gets, he's the enforcer the shooter—Get him before he gets you!"

"Yeah, I figured that. I also figure I'll get him best by way of his girl friend Susan."

"His girl friend? He has no friends.He'll blow her away as soon as he's through with her,"cautioned Al.

"Check him out first," his uncle urged "Know what you're running up against."

"Don't worry, unc. I'll do my homework—then I'll get him. I know I have to move fast. He'll probably be the very last guy the DEA goes after. They want the king pins, the ring leaders, to start with."

Upon leaving the hospital, Joe went back to his bachelor apartment and made some calls. The first was to McKay who updated him on the arrest of Nancy and her accomplices. He was assured all went well and that Nancy was already behind bars and still hysterical. After showering and shaving Joe placed a call to Sarah. His last contact with her lingered on. He could still smell her perfume when he dashed from her door to help his uncle as what seemed to be Susan looked on in the background.

But he also recalled that although Sarah was warm and huggable and turned him on, she seemed to have a strained smile—as though something was troubling her…something she wanted to tell him about but couldn't.

As he dialed the sisters' phone number, his mind flashed back again to his hurried exit from their house. He admitted to himself he should have prolonged the hugs and kisses and would have if it wasn't for his rush to help his uncle. Maybe she was irritated that he ran off so soon.

The voice on the phone was warm and sensuous but even more strained and different. "Sarah," asked Joe, "Sarah is that you?"

"Yes, I've been waiting for your call," was the response. He hesitated, wondering if Sarah had a cold. "You fighting the flu or something?" he asked.

"I'm almost over it now. But it's not contagious. It's left me a little hoarse, though. I'm sorry your uncle died." Joe was surprised since he told Sarah he was on his way to see Al who was feeling better. "Unc is okay. I got the antidote to him in time. Listen Sarah, and please—don't say anythng to your sister I've got to see you—tonight! It's very important. It has to do with Susan and the narc ring."

"Tonight Joe?" There was a pause which gave Susan just enough time to glance at Frank Meyers and get the nod to meet the cop. "Sure—your place or mine." Susan winked at her boyfriend and got another reassuring shake of his head.

"Good. I'll see you in half an hour at your place.—Remember, not a word to anyone about our getting together. And don't forget...I love you."

"He loves me—how about that," laughed Susan hanging up and removing the hanky helping to disguise her voice on the phone. "How can you hurt anyone who loves me, Frank?" She mused, "I guess I can still imitate sister Sary. But what does he know about me?"

Doesn't matter. The sucker,he's playing right into our hands," said Meyers. "He'll be here soon, so I'll leave. But I want you to find out everything he knows about the narc run. See if he'll tell you any more about the money Doc Klein snatched."

Meyers continued, "Whatever you do—don't tell him where Sarah is. We've got to keep her locked up in that room until we can find out what they've both been up to. We've gotta protect our ass, Sue. They can put us away for keeps. Don't worry about Sarah I won't hurt her. I want that money."

While this conversation was going on, Joe was still scratching his head wondering just who the hell he had been talking to. His cop sense may have been helping him load his gun again. That voice on the other end of the phone had all the inflections of Sarah's, but it lacked sincerity. Above all, Sarah never would have hung up without saying "I love you, too."

As Joe drove up to the sisters' modest little bungalow off one of the busy streets leading downtown, he noticed a dim light in a basement window of the house. He threw a jacket on over his gun strap and sauntered up to the door. Before knocking, he instinctively put his ear to the door as if to hear what was going on behind it.

The door quickly opened, showing what seemed to be Susan in a very transparent nightie. "Hi—let's go out tonight Joe. I've been in the house too long. I'll get dressed and we can relax and take it easy."

"Good idea...this house always seems so confining," remarked Kavinsky."Are you alone?" he asked looking about.

"Why do you ask? there's just the two of us. Susan's out with her girl friends again."

While Joe was at this doorway, Adel Sims was walking to her fancy door responding to the chimes she and the judge had spent so much for while overseas shopping. Upon opening the door slightly, Frank Meyers bolted against it and pushed himself inside the Sims mansion.

"I need those numbers, lady, and I need them fast." Meyers growled at the startled widow.

"I have no idea what you're talking about. Please leave at once!"

"Oh, I think you do, honey. I'm told you knew damn well that the judge was laundering crack money on the islands. Someone was onto this besides Doc Klein, and I have a good idea that someone is you. We couldn't find that key with those numbers in your home, but Klein probably got them through you. You knew that coroner DeSantro quite well didn't you?"

"Well—didn't you?" Meyers' whole being seemed enraged at this point and completely out of control.

"You're a mad man. I don't know what you're talking about. Now get out!"

"Well try this one on, honey. You staged that whole bit about the theft at your house to get the police off your trail. You also tipped off Lawrence at the fitness club that your husband was on the way. It was you that alerted Nancy Klein that he was wearing special red trunks you bought him the night before and that he had that knife with him in his bag.

"Everyone was well informed so they had no trouble knocking off your poor, trusting husband."

"You have no proof of that. Now get out at once or I'll call the police."

"Oh no! Perhaps you'd like to listen to the audio tape made when you phoned Klein and Lawrence. We've got it all down, baby, even your conversations with my boss Sapel about how you'd share in the take.

"Besides, Nancy did a double-cross Just like she did on DeSantro. She wasn't even thinking about giving you a cut, was she? Instead she was going to take it all. Can't you figure it out? You made a copy of the numbers, but you didn't figure DeSantro would get them first while examining your dead husband." He added, "DeSantro gave the cop wrong numbers and took off for the island banks—if he gave him any numbers at all. Only Nancy had other plans. If you have the numbers we can at least alert the island bankers, they'll put a stop on the payout. The drugs are coming in, but there's no one getting paid—at least no one I know. Nancy's in jail and Sapel is out for revenge. He'll kill you if you don't come through."

"And that's what you're here for?"

"Yes, for either the numbers…or your life."

"I've given them to Kavinsky," the widow said coldly.

"You're lying! you bitch," bellowed the enraged enforcer.

"No, it's true He was just here weeks before you came. He was wondering why my house was ramsacked. He had the same idea as you and Sapel, only he was going to give them to the DEA. I'd do anything to get back at my husband. I hated my husband He was cruel. I wanted to hurt him—terribly. Believe me, the cop knows about the numbers—everything."

"You're lying again. You're all trying to cut me out of the action. I do the dirty work and everyone else gets the cash is that how it is?" Meyers seized Mrs. Sims by the throat and began shaking her as if she could cough up the truth.

"No, I swear that young cop Kavinsky has what you want—He knows about you, Nancy, the judge—believe me," she pleaded gasping.

"Why should I? You're nothing but a damn liar." The enforcer tightened his hold around her neck until she went limp. He was careful, however, that she was still breathing enough to accept the injection he then administered into her arm. He knew what he was doing since it was the same injection he gave Alice Crimmons a few months ago in her garage.

Meyers then carried the small woman into the home's attached garage, placed her in the driver's seat of her husband's new Mercedes and turned the engine on. He locked the garage and made sure everything looked as though the widow, depressed over her husband's death, did herself in.

He looked at his watch on the way out the back door, wondering how Susan was doing with the cop who the enforcer was now more than ever determined to blow away.

CHAPTER 21

Although as beguiling as she was seductive, Susan wasn't completely outsmarting Kavinsky. He suspected that the woman he was talking to may really be his girl friend's identical twin.He figured he'd go along with her charade until he knew for certain Sarah's plight especially regarding where was she?and how could he help her?

Susan meanwhile was making the most out of the situation. She led him onto her couch and began stroking the shock of hair on the back of his neck near his open collar. Smiling, she looked away from his eyes as if he might detect the slightest difference in her pupils from those of her sister's.

Joe caught this distant look and put his head on her shoulder to encourage more conversation. "There's something wrong, I can see it in your eyes. Tell me, is everything all right? You seem very troubled.

"And where is your sister? Is she okay?" He continued prodding her to respond. Susan hesitated, as though trying to decide what to say and to speak carefully. This gave Joe the chance to add, "you girls always seem so close, so protective of one another. I'm sure neither of you would dare expose the other to danger."

He sensed that he was getting through Susan's masquerade. He knew that deep in her heart she was very fond of who she sometimes called her "baby sister." Noting this, he added, "your mother sure raised you girls right. You have always watched out for one another and have always helped each other along the way."

That seemed to do it. He could see tears beginning to appear at the edge of Susan's eyes. She took out her hanky and dabbed at them. But this impassioned scene was suddenly interrupted by the ringing of the nearby phone. The ringing seemed extra loud and annoying to Joe's ears since he sensed that Susan was already at that point to break down and start telling him the things he needed to hear.

Susan spoke so softly to the person on the other end of the line that Joe could hardly make out a word even though he was next to her. He figured, however, that the caller may be Frank since Susan's reaction was rather lukewarm just after listening to Joe bestow the virtues about her family ties with her mom and sister and protecting one another from harm.

Maybe this strategy was working after all, he thought. Maybe Susan was finally feeling a bit remorseful. Hopefully, he got her started on a guilt trip that could lead to some answers about what was going on in this rather spooky old house.

Frank was also speaking softly as though someone was with him in his car. He was alone, however, talking on his car phone as he sped through a suburb lined with shops. He cursed each time he had to stop for a red light as road rage began to engulf him. It was difficult driving since, despite being only late November, patches of ice and snow already were on the streets.

"Susan, keep that cop occupied. I was going to blow him away at your place but I don't think I should because your sister's in the house and he might find her first."

Susan gasped as Frank continued, "listen, and keep your mouth shut. Is it okay to talk?" When he got a frightful yes, he added, "tell him I'm at the harbor at Lake Calhoun, at the end of Lake Street. Let him know I'm waiting for him and will tell him everything he wants to know about the mob, the narc ring—everything."

He added, "I'll meet him there in a few minutes. This lets you go without having to give him any information. And tell him to come alone, without any police, and not to say anything to anybody or the deal's off—and I'll kill his girl friend. Okay, got it? And for your own good and your sister's don't screw up!"

Meyers snuffed out his cigarette and hung up without waiting for a reply. He patted his loaded Uzi on his lap and figured it would fit well under the belt of the snowmobile gear he had in the back seat of his car.

Susan put down the receiver with a frown on her face. She said nothing for a minute or two, as though digesting what Frank had said and not liking it. Her frown increased as she turned slowly toward Kavinsky.

"That bastard…that cold-hearted bastard," she said nearly screaming.

Joe figured this was a good time to move in. "What's up?" Why so mad?" he asked as casually as possible knowing that she was both angered and frustrated by the caller.

"He's rotten to the core that's what," Susan said as tears now streamed down her face. "And I won't let him get away with it. And to think I trusted him."

These were sweet words to Kavinsky. Perhaps now Susan would 'fess up to what's really going on, he hoped.

"He's going to hurt and maybe even do away with her—and you," she exclaimed, putting her hand to her mouth as if to silence herself. But it was too late. Joe sat upright and took her by the shoulders looking straight in her eyes.

"What's happening—Susan?" he almost shouted out her name to let her know he realized who she really is. "You're not fooling anyone You know damnwell where Sarah is don't you? And you know what Frank's planning to do next?"

"For God's sake—for your mother's sake,let me know what's going on so I can help you and Sarah. Meyers is a hired killer who won't stop at anything. He'll kill you in the same horrible way he's been killing the others. You've got to talk to me about this. I can help,believe me," Joe beseeched.

"She's down in the basement—locked in the old coal chute," was Susan's surprising response.

"Frank tied her up and threw her in there the other day when you came back. He said he wanted to break her down and wouldn't hurt her. He just wanted to frighten her to find out all he could about what you knew and where he could get those bank numbers for that laundered drug money.

"I went along with things. I didn't know he had anything to do with those killings—especially with my mother's death," Susan said defensively. "He was going to make me rich. He was going to cut me in on everything and daddy would be happy."

"It's too late for that now" Joe admonished as he grabbed Susan by the wrist and marched her down the basement steps to rescue Sarah. "Where's the key to that room?" he demanded as they almost ran to the coal chute bin.

"It's hidden in daddy's old tool box on his work bench. You'll find it under the electric drill and buzz saw. Frank put lots of newspapers around it." Instead of taking time to search for the key, Kavinsky ran to the shed.

He banged on the door of the old wooden shed, yelling: "Sarah, Sarah honey…it's Joe…we're coming. Are you okay? Can you hear me, are you okay?"

Getting no answer, he quickly rummaged through the tool box, finally finding the small key in a corner of the box wrapped in black paper. He almost stiffed-armed Susan in his attempt to get the key in the lock.

"This damn thing doesn't fit," he bellowed impatiently as Susan straightened her blouse from the slight impact with the cop.

"Here, you have to know how to do it. Daddy turned the key just half-way to open it...like this, she said, giving the rusty key a gentle nudge. There—it should open now with a slight push."

With his police training, Kavinsky didn't just push against the door—he kicked it soundly until the handle broke off and flew against the bin's cylinder block foundation.

The small window in the dark, dirty bin allowed a streak of sun light to peek in and led Joe to a huddled form lying in a corner. An unlit candle was on the window ledge as though put there intentionally, which may have been the reason for the slimmer of light he saw in the basement upon approaching the house. He ran quickly to the rescue. Lifting Sarah's head, he saw that she was breathing but that she had a large bump on her forehead and many bruises and abrasions on her neck and around her darkened eyes.

"It was Frank. He tried to get her to talk about your investigation. He roughed her up—I told him not to," explained Susan. Joe carried the limp form upstairs to the couch. After applying cold applications to her face and giving her some strong coffee, Sarah began moaning and coming around.

"Good, she's going to be okay. No thanks to that son-of-a-bitch Meyers," said Joe, while taking Sarah's pulse. "Call 911,' he demanded of Susan. "Tell them to get here immediately. Sarah needs some emergency room help."

Susan hesitated, as though in shock by all these dramatic and sudden events. This gave Joe the chance to add: "Where did Meyers want to meet me and when?"

"In a few minutes...at Lake Calhoun That's all he said. He promised to give you all the information you want, but I wouldn't believe him."

"Uh huh," muttered an unbelieving Kavinsky. "all I really want is him...I want him real good."

Shortly after Susan called 911, paramedics arrived and carried Sarah out the door on a stretcher. Susan promised Joe she would accompany her sister to the hospital and wait for his arrival there after his meeting with Meyers. Joe realized this could take a long time.

CHAPTER 22

As Joe sped to the lake he noticed snow lightly falling on his windshield again. It appeared that a storm was brewing to add more flakes to the many already on the ground. Winter often lasted through April in Minnesota and could be near its peak already in late fall. But he also knew that sun and high temps the past few days made lakes risky, leaving spaces called black holes in the ice.

The snow became heavier with twilight nearing and Joe's vision became somewhat blurred by fog and flakes. He drove around the long lake twice searching for Meyers while trying to listen to police radio reports as his loud windshield wipers streaked his windshield. One report was interrupted by a news flash about an accident at the Executive Workout Club. A receptionist, Lillian Norton, was found dead on a ledge overlooking the pool. She apparently stumbled and fell from the top floor and her head struck the ledge. Police were at the site still investigating.

While Joe scoffed, figuring Lillian was pushed off because she knew too much, he turned on his squad car light to let Meyers know he was looking for him. Moments later he spotted a guy in a long coat waiving on a deserted beach. He parked and tried to get across the snowy lawn to reach the waving person, but by the time he was half-way, Frank was in his snowmobile gunning the engine.

Kavinsky looked around desperately to find another snowmobile to pursue him. Recalling his days as a boy at the beach, Joe knew there may be a snowmobile in the maintenance shed under the gazebo which was, fortunately, nearby. Meanwhile, he could hear Frank's snowmobile racing toward the middle of the lake.

The maintenance shed, unfortunately, was locked. The old padlock was encased with ice and snow. Not wanting to alert Meyers of his whereabouts, Joe was reluctant to blow up the lock by shooting at it. He ran nearly around the shed before spotting a window Using the butt of his gun, he reached up and smashed the window and looked for a box or some other object which he could stand on to reach the window frame,enabling him to slide through the window and into the shed. He noticed a box near the water pump at the entrance to the beach house and quickly put it under the window ledge.

He could hear himself grunt and strain as he got on the wooden box and struggled to wiggle into the small window opening. Although mainly concerned about trying to get his legs over the window frame, he wondered why he couldn't hear Frank's snowmobile motor any more. At this point, his body was nearly all the way through the window opening. He jumped inside and landed in a kneeling position on the cold cement floor of the old shed.

With a penlight as a flashlight, he quickly looked about for some sort of a hanging light bulb he could turn on to hopefully find a park snowmobile that was gassed up and ready to go. He nearly gave up when he caught sight of a large object in one corner covered with canvas.

The object at first looked square, but after closer scrutiny Joe could make out some handle bars sticking out from the canvas. He rapidly removed the canvas cover and discovered a relatively new streamlined snowmobile bearing the name "Park Police" on its silvery side. Moreover, since it was a late model, Joe knew it had excellent acceleration, fast enough to help catch Meyers.

"But the keys—where the hell are the keys?" The cop yelled almost out-of-control as he frantically searched for the ignition keys to turn on the fancy snowmobile. He knocked things about and looked under and behind nearly every object in the tiny shed. After many minutes of this madness, his search was suddenly interrupted by a loud beeping noise. Startled somewhat, Joe stopped abruptly in his wild searching attempt before realizing the sound was coming from the pager's beeper on his belt. It told him to call a number at his police precinct.

"Yeah—who's there?" Joe almost bellowed into his cell phone in a voice mixed with exhaustion and impatience, knowing that the police would be the only ones able to tap into his pager.

"Joe—it's me, Dave Paulson. Where the hell are you? do you need any help? The guys at the precinct and I haven't seen you for a long time. What's up? Remember, we were supposed to be partners Joe—Joe can you hear me?"

"Dave—cool it will ya," assured Joe. "I'm okay, but I guess I could use some help. I'm running after Frank Meyers near the Calhoun Beach club. But I can't find the keys to the police snowmobile in this damn park maintenance shed."

There was a long pause before Paulson got back to Kavinsky. It was as though Paulson had another person in the room giving him advice.

"I'm told you can usually find those keys in a little package tied to the back of the steering post wheel," said Joe's annoying partner.

Kavinsky grabbed for the steering post and quickly felt around it until his fingers came on what seemed to be a tiny bag or envelope at the bottom and under the post. He got down on the floor of the machine and flashed his light up. By god, there it was—attached by wire around the metal post. With just a few twists of the wire band the envelope fell to the floor allowing Joe to reach inside for the elusive keys.

He then remembered that Paulson was still holding on waiting to hear from him. Grabbing the phone again, he informed Paulson that he found the keys and needed police backup to help him arrest Meyers.

"But come on him slowly and carefully. Surprise him. We'll need another snowmobile or so to catch up to him. Chances are, he wants to meet me on a pier to give me information—or kill me," warned Kavinsky.

Joe was surprised that no one responded. It was as though Paulson was cut off in the middle of his conversation. But Kavinsky didn't have time to figure this out. Instead, all he wanted to do at the moment was to get his damn machine going to wring Meyers' neck.

His urge for vengeance was thwarted, however, when he suddenly remembered there was only one door to drive the snowmobile out of and onto the frozen lake—and that was the one so tightly locked that he couldn't budge it. He realized there was only one way out—to smash through the wooden door with his snowmobile.

He clenched his teeth, blessed himself again knowing what the crash could do to him, covered his face with an elbow, lowered his head so it was protected behind the extra strong windshield, and pulled out the throttle. Nothing happened—just silence. Not even a slight murmur was heard to indicate that he was doing things right or that there was even an engine in the damn vehicle.

Joe stomped on the gas pedal, pushed the throttle in and out again, and angrily crouched over once more to cope with the expected engine roar and ultimate crashing of the door. Still nothing. Joe was beginning to feel like a fool in an old silent movie. He recalled this was how you usually started a snowmobile—at least the kind he drove as a kid around the farm. He began feeling cold and nervous as sweat formed on his forehead as he tried to figure out what the hell he was doing wrong. There must be some way to get this damn thing going.

Realizing that when everything else fails read the instructions, as his mother used to remind him, Joe looked about at the dashboard for any messages that might tell him how to operate this machine. However, there were no messages, labels, or user-guide booklets—not even the customary literature congratulating the driver on owning this new streamlined snowmobile model.

He finally noticed a key hole on the dash and wondered how he ever missed seeing this during all his frantic attempts. Joe blushed realizing he indeed was a fool, at least when it came to snowmobiles. Mad at himself he muttered out loud: "Put one of those keys you found in the hole, idiot."

By so doing, a mighty roar filled the quiet park maintenance shed. But he was so surprised and startled by the sudden noise, he forgot to push the throttle in immediately. This caused the engine to rev up so fast that the whole machine began vibrating violently, almost shaking the shed.

Realizing he must have his brakes on, Joe looked around and found what looked like an emergency brake handle. The instant he released the brake, the machine took off like the proverbial bat out of hell. It struck and destroyed the old wooden door in an instant, flinging slats around the entire shed and, due to the terrific force of the crash, caused some of the door's flying pieces to crack the snowmobile windshield.

It took a few moments for Joe's eyes to accommodate once he was outside. The sun came out,causing a brilliant glare from the snow and ice. The crack in the windshield added to his visual impairment. But his eyes finally focused and, as he looked around the windshield crack he discovered he was only seconds away from smashing into a giant elm tree on the slopes along the edge of the lake. Thanks to his training as a stock car racer during his high school years he was able to swerve just in time, but headed almost out of control down the slope and onto the ice of the lake.

He pulled in the throttle some more and the machine finally settled down. With the motor noise now significantly subdued, he could try to hear and look for Meyers around the spacious lake. But all he could see at first was white nothingness; a tundra, surrounded by trees bordering a huge body of frozen water. Joe stopped to observe and listen more closely.

The wind was beginning to howl as Joe sped through the blowing snow squinting to see what was in his path. It was then that he heard what seemed to be a horn in the distance—a snowmobile horn. Peering through the snow piling up on his windshield, he could barely make out the form of a snowmobile on the horizon and a lone person sitting in it. Yes, there was Frank—many yards away, almost exactly at the center of the lake.

He responded by sounding his horn. The echo seemed to bounce around the lake. Again, the other horn was heard, like a signal for him to come—and trust the fate that awaited him. The cop gunned up his engine again, this time pulling out the throttle all the way, and eased off on the brake. He accelerated quickly from 15 to 45 miles-per-hour, keeping his eyes on the ice at all times. He knew from his childhood days on this lake that it could have some very big holes in the winter, large enough to swiftly swallow up an unaware snowmobile driver and entomb him under its solid surface.

As Kavinsky rapidly drove to the waiting snowmobile he once more put his small pistol together and placed it under his cap. He wasn't sure what to expect when he met Meyers, but, like the proverbial Canadian mounted police, he was determined to bring back his man.

CHAPTER 23

Kavinsky had to steer around several holes to get to the middle of the lake, but he finally reached Meyers who had climbed on a diving platform and stood there with a smirk on his face when Joe pulled up. However, much to Joe's surprise, Frank also had an Uzy in his hands. There was no escape, Joe could be blown away even if he was only 20 yards away and if Frank was a poor shooter.

The cop blamed himself for not noticing the high-powered automatic gun from a distance,but figured Meyers must have had it slung behind his back before Joe drove up. Admitting that this was another foolish move on his part, he realized it was too late to do anything about it. That type gun, complete with scope, could have riddled his snowmobile and his entire body in only seconds from the time Joe started driving on the ice. But why didn't he use it then? Joe wondered. Apparently he wanted to contact Joe eye-ball to eye-ball and personally question him about something.

"Howdy cop, I've been waiting for you," drawled Meyers with a scowl.

"You wanted to talk with me...to get some information, remember Frank? You can't do that if you use that gun on me," responded a nervous Kavinsky.

"All I really want from you are those numbers, cop, the numbers DeSantro gave to you. Old lady Sims didn't have them. She said you knew all about them."

Seeing a way to buy time, Kavinsky thought up a quick lie, "You'll have to go back to the swim club I've got them posted inside my locker. No one knows."

You can remember them,and you know it. Tell me the numbers now or you're one dead cop Kavinsky. I've killed for these and you'll be just one more notch on my gun." With that, Meyers cocked the weapon and pointed it directly at Joe's chest.

"No, trust me Frank. I'll take you to the numbers. There's probably no one in the locker room this late in the day. No one has to know. I'll simply pass them on to you," Joe tried to explain.

"Give me the locker combination and I'll do it myself. You must know that,even cops aren't that dumb," sneered the dope dealer as he pointed the muzzle of his assault weapon up and down, from Joe's feet to his head

Kavinsky knew he was stopped in his lie. If he told Meyers he couldn't remember, Frank would probably realize that he was bluffing and stalling for time. If he told him the locker combination and Frank really believed him, he would be shot for sure figuring he no longer needs the cop.

About his only defense was to stammer, as he did when he was a kid flustered with a question from a teacher.He was so nervous at this point that he honestly couldn't remember his locker combination. It sounded very convincing as he tried to make up some combination. "O-o-o-okay, F-f-f-frank," Joe stuttered, "But quit aiming that gun at me. I believe they're 0-34-56 and uh-uh—there's two more numbers but I just can't remember them. Your gun is causing me to be confused. Please put the damn thing to one side. I'm sure I won't be so nervous and can remember lots better."

"If you're up to some tricks, cop, I'll blow your goddam head off right here. I'll give you a few more minutes to remember. If you don't, I'll personally go to your locker and knock the lock off, okay?. But then again, how do I know you're leveling with me? You must know the number on your locker you dumb asshole."

"I don't—they're not numbered. What do you have to lose Frank by taking me with you? The club receptionist has been killed, she can't give you them. There's no one in the club that knows the location of my locker. Hell, you can shoot me after you get the numbers," he said, hardly believing these foolhardy words were coming from his mouth

"I haven't even checked you out yet, Kavinsky. You're probably hiding a gun. Raise your arms and spread your legs—if we go anywhere you're not going to be carrying a weapon." Meyers reached over and began patting Kavinsky's pants legs, arms and chest in search of any hidden weapon.

"Trust me Frank," said Joe, as Meyers poked his Uzy in the cop's back forcing him to cooperate in the search.

"Shut up. You're just lucky I've let you live this long you son-of-a-bitch."

After making sure the cop was clean, he raised his gun to Joe's head. "You're as crazy as I thought. You're not even carrying a gun. Did you think we were going to have a tea party out here you stupid bastard?"

He moved the Uzy again, pointing it once more at Joe's head. "About the only place I haven't looked is under your cap," said Meyers. "But it would have to be pretty small, considering the size of your brain," he said, chuckling nervously.

"Take it off!" commanded Meyers getting impatient. "Take off that cap!"

Joe was shocked by this order. He wasn't sure what to do. If he hesitated or refused, Frank would suspect the worse. He automatically brought his arm up to carefully remove the cap, moving very slowly to provide him some time to figure out what his next step should be—or if indeed there would be any more steps for him.

But Meyers' attention was suddenly diverted at this point by what seemed to be the sound of another snowmobile. The noise of the snowmobile engine gradually increased and before Joe could continue to bring his hand to his cap, the strange snowmobile was in view and almost ready to join up with Frank.

"Who's that?" Joe said loudly, hoping this would help distract Meyers further.

"My friends. Just wait, cop, they'll make you talk plenty—very loudly and perhaps without a tongue."

Joe could see that the advancing snowmobile was specially designed and so large it could easily accommodate the three big men riding in it who seemed to be screaming and waving at Meyers. He also noticed that each had a ski mask on. And, as they got closer, he noticed that each also had a gun.

About the only possible support Joe had in all this terrifying scenario was in knowing that his tiny Derringer-type pistol was still undetected under his cap and hoping that the masked men were maybe really good cops.

But his hopes were dashed when the driver and the guy next to him removed their masks, revealing the grinning faces of Andy Sapel and Dr. John Loring. He was further depressed when the other guy removed his mask, disclosing the homely face of Paulson. All seemed pleased with their arrival, already savoring the elimination of their chief irritant—the ever-pursuing police lieutenant.

"Surprise! surprise!—You gave me all the information I needed to find you," greeted Paulson. "I brought along some of your other buddies. The chief apologizes he couldn't make it, he had some more important matters to take care of. You know, embezzlements and things like that." Paulson couldn't help but laugh at what he was saying.

His other two companions didn't say a word. Instead, they beckoned Meyers to get in their snowmobile. With guns pointed on him, Joe sat in the middle of this deadly foursome while they headed farther out in the lake until reaching another swimming platform.

Meyers still had his Uzy trained on Kavinsky as he shoved him up the steps to the top of the 5-ft. tall platform. The structure was designed mostly for kids who enjoyed plunging into the waters of the cold and historic lake during the summer months when Calhoun attracts hundreds of Twin Citians to its beaches. For years that lake was out-of-bounds for motor boats of any kind. Until only recently, the only craft allowed on the lake were for sailing. The city fathers wished to assure that this charming, peaceful body of water, bordered by expensive homes, would forever be free of any loud boating noise for the pleasure and serenity of those concerned about protecting the beauty of the lake and environment.

When this crowd of snowmobile occupants reached the platform landing they pushed Kavinsky to a corner and Sapel gestured to Meyers to keep his weapon directed at the cop.

Lighting a cigarette, Sapel asked Joe if he wanted a smoke. The cop, pretending to be as agreeable as possible, nodded that he would and was quickly given the one already lit—pushed right into his face. Kavinsky screamed knowing that this was probably just the beginning of his torture.

"You're going to tell us all we want to know Kavinsky. If you're lucky—and play ball with us, you may walk away from this yet. If not, you'll be playing ball with the fishes down below. You've been a thorn in our sides for too long. We think you know how we can still get our money from that big haul you helped to bring in from the Bahamas."

Joe forced a smile, remembering his childhood days when playing sandlot baseball with some of the bullies around his tough neighborhood. His buddies had an old saying about their opponents that went something like this: "if you play ball with these guys you'll probably end up having the bat jammed down your throat."

"Let me at him, he'll tell us what we want—fast," broke in Meyers impatiently. "I can show him some real police brutality," he laughed. But it was Loring who caught everyone's attention when he drew out what appeared to be an inoculation needle. "A little of this might also do wonders gents," he announced.

"Is that the same needle used on poor old Alice Crimmons and the judge?" asked Joe as he struggled to escape from the others who were holding him down.

"You're very observing," remarked the medical examiner. "But you and your uncle were always too nosy for your own good, weren't you?" The doctor continued, "The serum in this should help you remember everything you know about us. It won't hurt much. Just relax and let the needle do the work."

To defend himself, Joe turned his head and lifted his arms to ward off the needle. As he was looking back squirming he noticed what seemed to be a rare winter "sailboard", a craft specially made to travel on ice. It appeared to be quietly and quickly approaching. Such ice boats are often used for special exhibitions during the winter on Twin Cities lakes since they can accelerate very swiftly across frozen water with only a little push from the wind and—best of all—they're completely silent.

Realizing time was precious, Kavinsky turned back to his tormentors without mentioning what he had seen through the mist on the watery horizon. "Wait doc—do you really want to be a cop killer? You may only get a few words from me and I'd be dead. I know this for a fact. The physicians warned me about my allergy to this during my police academy training."

Loring hesitated, still holding the needle. "If you know this will kill you, then you had better start informing us about what we want to know, Kavinsky. Otherwise I'm going to jab you and you can take the risks. You can't afford to be risky—this serum will lower your immune system too much."

"What do you want to know and who are you kidding Loring? you already know all the answers. You already know damn well that you pulled a switch on your partner Doc DeSantro and have those bank numbers. But maybe your friend Sapel doesn't know about that though?"

"You're crazy. You don't know what you're talking about." Caught off guard, Loring looked wildly around to see Sapel's reaction. What he saw was a puzzled sneering face with cold, distrustful inquiring eyes.

"Don't believe him Andy. I had nothing to do with that. DeSantro was suppose to give you the numbers."

"But he didn't, did he," snarled Sapel. "Maybe the cop knows what he's talking about. It would have been much easier and better for you to use the numbers for you and your girl friend Nancy. Yeah—I'll bet that's why you blew him up over the ocean, nice and clean—no evidence at all."

Sapel added with a scowl, "You spent some time with Nancy in the Bahamas, didn't you doc, I found that out just after DeSantro's accident. You two probably planned this whole thing."

Taken back by this sudden turn of events, Loring responded in a nervous, almost panic voice, "You're as crazy as the cop. Let me give him this shot, we'll learn the truth."

"Yeah—and you'll kill the truth. I'll be dead and Sapel still won't know if he can trust you," interrupted Kavinsky taking advantage of Sapel's reaction to all this.

"He's right—don't touch him with that!" ordered Sapel. "I suppose you'd like him dead to shut him up for your own good wouldn't you doc?"

"Don't be an ass, Sapel—why would I be afraid of what he has to say? He's lying to save his skin."

"Sure," agreed Sapel still scowling. "And you may be, too."

With this, the frustrated Loring yelled and ran with the needle toward Joe who stuck his foot out to trip him. The mad doctor didn't notice the foot, causing him to stumble and fall on the wet floor of the platform. The floor was so slippery that Loring couldn't stop and quickly slid off the platform, striking his head on one of the railings. As blood oozed from his head, Loring fell into the swirling circle of water surrounding the gurgling, melting ice surrounding a post supporting the platform.

"Sapel, I can't swim, I can't swim," the frantic medical examiner screamed.

"Good, maybe you know now how the judge felt going down," Sapel yelled back smiling at the struggling, drowning doctor. Loring's head seemed to bob up and down with the motion of the now turbulent water of the lake as the waves became stronger. He finally sank out of sight as the others watched in awe, nervous over Sapel's cold-blooded attitude and how it could be used on them.

Sapel broke the silence. "You're next cop. What do you know about us? You did lots of research, I'm sure. I'll give you only a few more minutes to talk, if not you'll be as dead as Loring."

"But not as dead as you'll be Sapel if you don't lower that gun," rang out a voice that Joe had heard many times before. The words bellowed from a man wearing a DEA cap and aiming a super powerful "cannon" directly at Sapel's torso. Before even looking at the guy with the gun, Joe knew who was holding it. "Terry—my guardian angel. You were following me all this time?" His buddy drug-buster tipped his cap and looked back sternly at the trio with their arms up. They all dropped their weapons on seeing his AK-47 aimed at them. They knew that a burst would quickly cut them down.

CHAPTER 24

"Where the hell did you come from?" asked the surprised Sapel holding his arms up high.

"From my special sailboard that you couldn't hear," replied Johnson, still waiving his automatic weapon that resembled a bazooka. "Just one little movement and I'll blow you into the sunset gentlemen," warned Joe's comrade from the islands

"You came alone?" asked Joe, puzzled over the apparent foolhardy bravery of Terry.

"Well, not quite. I had some help from your partner here," said Johnson—pointing to Paulson, who had dropped his gun by his side and was grinning like a proud kid.

"Who the hell do you suppose tipped him off wise guy," shrugged Paulson. "I was told to keep an eye on you and by god I did. I was under-cover and was praying Johnson would hurry up."

Kavinsky found it difficult to believe that Paulson could ever be on the good-guy side. All along, he felt Dave was nothing but a phony in cahoots with the chief. At times, he almost felt embarrassed in even knowing this detective who compiled such a bad reputation as being a "hot shot" on the force. Never for an instant did he think Paulson would come to his rescue.

As all this was going on, however, Frank Meyers was nudging up closer to the edge of the platform. It wasn't until too late that Johnson,

Kavinsky and Paulson noticed that Frank was about to leap off. His big body struck the ice where it was still quite solid and only a few feet from his waiting snowmobile. He grimaced in pain, holding his leg.

Before anyone could use their weapons to stop him, however, Frank was off and fleeing on the snowmobile. Feeling foolish, the police trio simply looked guilty at one another wondering what to do next as they stood watching Meyers fading away on the lake now being engulfed in heavy fog.

"He won't get very far I think he injured his leg when he hit the ice," remarked Paulson.

"Don't count him out, he's swifter than you think," said Joe. "I'm going after him. You fellas take care of Sapel. And you better call for help to get Loring's body."

"Be careful Joe...that guy's extra strong and mean," cautioned Terry.

"I know," Joe said as he hopped onto his snowmobile. "But he has to go slow in this soup or he'll end up in the water for sure."

"There's giant holes around that part of the lake where he's heading," Paulson shouted down to him. "I almost ran into them getting here."

Joe shrugged and turned the engine on. Intent on running Meyers down, he accelerated the throttle and sped toward what appeared to be a wall of fog still filled with the strong and smelly exhaust from Meyer's overheated engine.

As Joe entered this hazy mist, he looked from side to side to see if Meyers was waiting to pounce on him, although he knew Frank had dropped his weapon before fleeing and wasn't armed. Joe's engine noise grew louder as he roared farther and farther into a section of the lake unknown to him. But he could at least make out some markers and knew he was passing from Calhoun into Cedar Lake and if the chase continued he soon would be entering several other connecting lakes.

To hear better, the cop turned off his engine and listened intently to detect any sound of Meyers' engine. He finally heard what sounded like a motor sputtering and knew he wasn't far from Frank. However, he also realized Frank could have turned down the engine volume to help reduce the noise.

But realizing Frank's engine noise could be deceptive, Kavinsky knew Frank could really be only a few yards from him or as far away as a mile or so. It was too risky to make any assumptions. He figured Meyers was probably a great swimmer, having worked out daily at the club, and could probably force the cop under the ice and drown him if he caught him by surprise.

Feeling his cap again, and the gun underneath, Joe took the gun, checked to see if it was loaded, and got out of the snowmobile. He decided to walk. It would be safer that way—from two standpoints: he wouldn't be running into any hidden ice holes and he could be especially quiet and prepared if Frank was waiting to surprise him.

Darkness was closing in fast along as the fog became more dense. The sun had already set and only the Minnesota loon, the state's official bird, broke the evening's strange silence with its lonely mating calls. As Joe carefully walked into this, he felt almost like a sitting duck. It was worse than walking through a cemetery at midnight, he thought, recalling his scary days as a boy doing Halloween pranks. At least you had some grave stones to hide behind.

The distant engine noise could be heard more clearly now as he proceeded ahead. It was almost helping him find his way to Frank. Suddenly he felt his feet getting wet. Without a flashlight, Joe had no idea if he was walking into a hole or just stepping into some slush. If a hole was in front of him, he could expect to be wallowing about in freezing water very soon and groping for whatever edge of ice he could grasp before falling into the lake. But the ice probably would be so thin that it wouldn't hold him up.

Instinctively he backed up, and kept doing so until his feet began feeling dry. Since the surface seemed solid at this point, he veered sharply to the right and kept walking very lightly,almost tip-toeing,in case it got wet again or if he would hear any cracking of ice beneath him.

Meyers' snowmobile engine now could be heard louder and more clearly. Joe's hand tightened on his little pistol as his body tensed knowing that danger was also getting closer. He could hear his own nervous breathing, almost in sync with the sound of the engine.

He also suddenly heard a rustle, a movement—coming directly toward him. Joe could still see nothing. He looked directly ahead and couldn't detect anyone or anything, not even a hint of either the snowmobile or the driver.

He was caught nearly completely off guard. In fact, he would never have heard the sound behind him if Frank, who was sneaking up on Joe, hadn't slipped into a melting sludge of ice causing the burly gunman to curse. Whirling around, Kavinsky saw the wild-eyed man about to crush his skull with a snowmobile tire wrench.

Kavinsky quickly reacted using the martial arts skills he learned at the police academy. Rather than turning to face his attacker, he leaped and kicked his legs out in front of the advancing Frank. One foot caught Meyers squarely on the jaw, causing him to drop the tire wrench as he fell hard on the ice from the blow.

But this only stirred up greater rage in the already crazed drug addict bent on murder. He quickly got up and ran again toward the cop. This time, however, Kavinsky missed with his reverse jump-and-strike defense. Instead Meyers was able to grab Joe's foot and twist it, causing the cop to strike his head against the ice. Joe could only see stars at this point but knew Meyers was standing over him ready for the kill.

Still holding the pistol he had been hiding, Kavinsky could only make out the form of what appeared to be a enraged giant holding a wire to strangle him. To further complicate his vision, he only saw a double, blurred image of his attacker hovering over him and wondered which image he should be shooting at—and why were there so many Franks fluttering all around him?

Unfortunately, he had to wait for his head to clear before pulling the trigger even though his assailant was ready to pounce on him. It was crucial that his aim was accurate since he'd only have one chance to stop him. If he missed...the wire would be around Joe's neck.

Frank did the expected, he flung his body on the cop in an attempt to restrain him as he went for Joe's throat with the wire. Kavinsky gasped as Meyers landed on top of him, and almost lost his grasp of the pistol from the heavy impact. He brought the gun up, but not before Meyers noticed it.

Frank dropped the wire and leaped for the gun. The two struggled desperately in an attempt to seize the tiny weapon. Sensing the right time to give Frank a kick in the groin, Kavinsky bent his knees and kicked out hard with both feet. He could hear Meyers groan and knew the kick must have hit him in the balls. This gave the cop the chance to aim his gun at one of Meyers' waving arms. He quickly pulled the trigger.

Frank rolled off the cop as fast as the melting ice rapidly dripped from the edge of the black hole near their struggle. He covered his bleeding arm with one hand, cursing Joe almost spasmodically and shook his fist with the other. He rose quickly, however, much faster than Joe could react, and hobbling, bleeding and still cursing ran off to his snowmobile nearby and turned on the engine.

"Frank, don't!"...hollered Kavinsky, realizing Meyers was planning to drive wildly away with the use of only one arm. "There's too many holes. You'll never make it."

Ignoring Joe's warning, however, Meyers opened the throttle all the way and gunned the engine. He didn't even look back as he roared off from his pursuer. He sped off so fast, in fact, that Joe almost lost sight of the drug enforcer who was fading swiftly away over the horizon still yelling as Kavinsky slowly stood up. His head still spinning, Joe was impressed by everything being suddenly silent, no engine noise, no yelling, no nothing. Instead, all he heard were sounds of splashing water which replaced the loud struggling and snowmobile noise.

Joe ran to where he thought the splashing was coming from, but couldn't find any trace of either snowmobile or driver. After carefully approaching a large black hole where the water seemed to be gurgling, he spotted what appeared to be something or someone floating to the top. He stood near the hole wondering how he might be of help.

It was then that Frank suddenly bobbed to the surface and reached out for Joe. His hand came out of the water and seized the cop's leg, although it was weak the hand held tight like a death grip. Despite trying to shake it loose, the hand tightened as if determined to hang on through all eternity. Joe began slipping toward the hole with each yank from this hand of death.

There was only one thing to do, thought Joe. To avoid drowning with Meyers, the cop pressed his pistol next to the desperate hand and pulled the trigger. Blood spurted out from the hand wound, with much of it splashing on Kavinsky's jacket. Some flowed back into the water as the anguished Meyers screamed and released his hold on Joe's leg.

Kavinsky tried to reach out for Frank who was now floating submerged toward the middle of the hole. Joe looked around for a long pole or stick that Meyers could grab onto. Joe removed his jacket and, with one hand holding a sleeve of the jacket, flung it to the struggling mobster. Meyers, exhausted from his struggles, tried grabbing the other sleeve of the jacket but missed. He then went under the water again and upon resurfacing tried one more futile attempt to grasp the jacket. But Joe knew this could be the last time Frank would appear when his chance to seize the jacket failed and he went under again screaming. The murky churning water seemed to turn calm in only a few minutes after Meyers didn't resurface, as if it was finally satisfied in swallowing up its notorious victim.

There was no longer anything Kavinsky could do. He removed his cap as a farewell gesture to the dead and began heading back toward the brighter side of the lake. The sounds of the loons became louder as he approached his snowmobile and a beautiful sunset began streaking through the clouds once more.

The cop carefully steered around the ice holes on his trip back to the diving platform and was relieved to see that Johnson, Paulson—and their prisoner Sapel were gone. If everything went well, he was certain that Andy was now behind bars. As he continued toward shore he felt rather guilty for apparently misjudging Paulson and that from now on he would try to trust his partners more.

Not bothering to store the snowmobile in the shed where he got it, Kavinsky jumped in his car and took off for his police precinct. Sure enough, Paulson and the DEA had Sapel safely put away. After recalling his struggles with Meyers and calling for an ambulance to visit the lake scene, Joe was informed by Terry that "It's only a matter of time before we have everyone connected with this drug ring in the slammer where they belong."

"Yes, but how much time? Can you imagine how many other casualties there will be if this continues?" Joe asked.

"We're already starting to round them all up, Joe. The FBI and other feds and local enforcers are helping us. Your Twin Cities is full of dope traffickers and so many are in very prestigious, protective places. We have to tred mighty softly to get them all. But thanks to you, we've already scored a big one by getting Sapel."

"And save your thanks until we have them all locked up behind bars—if we have enough bars," Joe responded thoughtfully. "That goes for all the other illegal drug traffickers—including those in the Mideast who are growing and dealing the stuff. They also have reps in the U.S. and I believe Judge Sims may have been connected with them, too, in paying and transporting. It's just that his Bahama connection got to him first. when they began to doubt his loyalties."

Paulson, with that silly grin on his face that Joe always disliked, put his arm around Kavinsky's shoulders as though they were now old buddies. Joe sort of pulled away at first, but then realized that he owed Dave one—and maybe lots more—for his help in bringing in Sapel and his pals.

"Your girl friend is okay, too, pardner," assured Paulson. "McKay said the paramedics took good care of her. She's back on her feet and real eager to hear from you."

"Uh—thanks Dave. In fact, thanks for all your help out there," although it was sort of like a kick in the groin for Joe to admit this. "Frankly, at one time I thought you were in with the chief and the others, that the only one I could really trust on the entire force was McKay."

"I know, Charley told me. He also filled me in on what was going on with you and Nancy Klein at the pool. I was real glad you called me when you did. I had no idea where you might be and who was out to hit on you. You probably know from Susan that Meyers also did away with Sims' wife."

Joe's surprise over this news was apparent. He could only mutter, "that damn bastard."

Paulson added, "McKay is healing well from that slug he got in the shoulder. It was just superficial. He should be back raising hell at the office again in a couple of weeks."

"Great!" exclaimed kavinsky, looking at his watch.

"I understand you can reach Sarah at her mom's old house," Paulson said with his silly grin upon noticing Joe's eagerness to rush off. "She's getting ready to close up the place."

Joe grinned back, with a wink of an eye.

"Gotta go," he said. "But first I better phone my uncle."

On only the second ring, Al Benjamin was on the phone at his newspaper office.

"Back at it again already unc?"

"Joey—where the hell have you been? Your aunt Kay and I were starting to check the obituary columns on you. How's it going? Have you brought any of them in yet?"

Kavinsky chuckled. "Always the reporter aren't you uncle Al."

"You know I'll never change Joey. Do you have any scoops for me? It's late, and we're going into our second run. Can we put those guys down yet on our front page?"

"Yes and maybe. There's lots to tell you: key names, business leaders,even DEA plans that could snatch Beck and the whole nine yards. But you'll have to wait a little longer 'till I check with my fiancee."

"Your what?"…gasped his startled uncle.

"Sarah—Sarah Crimmons. You remember her unc. I'm about to ask her for her hand. By the way, make sure aunt Kay is sitting down when you tell her this," said the bemused police lieutenant.

"We'll be sure to save a big space on the society page for that announcement," chuckled his uncle. "And, of course, we'll also save the front page for that story your bringing in on the state's biggest dope ring bust of the century."

CHAPTER 25

While Joe and Sarah were being toasted on their upcoming wedding at a pre-nuptial party in downtown Minneapolis, amid a romantic setting in the penthouse of the American Express tower, Terry Johnson and other DEA personnel were beginning to crash other type "parties" around the Twin Cities. Only these parties varied from settings in luxurious offices of very affluent executives to crowded and smelly backrooms of junkies counting their drug stuff and profits.

Drug traffickers hiding behind executive doors ranged from heads of major financial corporations to lawyers and police officials and many of their wealthy cronies. When necessary, the"party crashers", both local and federal law enforcers, almost crashed down the closed doors of the surprised suspects, but in most cases, especially the more dignified ones, they just paraded through their hallways, past their startled secretaries and banged loudly on executive doors. They allowed only seconds before kicking in the doors.

They went on their rounds guided by the list of suspects flown in by Terry Johnson who had noted their names, affiliations, and other pertinent information in his little "diary" he carried about under his belt during his undercover stay in Bimini.

One key player in all this exposed corruption was the CEO and president of the second-ranked major corporation in the Twin Cities metro area. He was secluded away on the top floor of his spacious computer headquarters, behind extra thick bullet-proof glass paneling installed a few years before when disgruntled employees were wondering why their wages were frozen and they were forced to work so many extra hours without pay. This happened to be during the time this same CEO was becoming involved with additional drug trafficking and was being pressured to have money forwarded to the drug lords.

When notified by security at the front door that uniform police were on the way to arrest him, he was already packing some of his highly-priced office memorabilia, including many exotic and expensive gifts from some of the numerous countries he visited while contacting drug lord pals. He was pre-warned that the cops may be getting closer many months before by Judge Sims.

When alerted about the raid, the CEO stopped packing and approached a large bay window at the side of his big desk. There was probably nothing he could do now to prevent being put behind bars, he thought. He then looked around the walls of his spacious office adorned with trophies, photos of himself with important people throughout the business world as well as those of his wife and family. There also were many mementos of his company sponsoring expensive events for "influential" customers, including many from the nation's capital.

He doubted now if any of these powerful "allies", including those he threw the most money to rather than spend it on his workers, could do anything at this point to help clear his name, especially to keep him from prison along with the many others on the DEA hit list.

For one moment, in his depressed state, he thought it best to throw himself out the window to the courtyard fifteen floors below where his employees trudged to work or carried picket signs. He opened the window and peered out, but despite outside noise he could still hear the loud talk and commotion increasing near his office doors, apparently from secretaries and others wondering about the sudden invasion of

police in the hallowed halls of this stately and highly restricted corporate executive area.

But even at this most desperate time the CEO couldn't bring himself
to jump. Although often risking his neck to deal with the drug world, he
was a coward inwardly. Instead, his clever mind protected him once
more by assuring that a man in his prestigious position could fight the
law. He figured he was untouchable—that is until Terry Johnson
touched him on a shoulder with a set of cold handcuffs.

The CEO turned abruptly, gazing defiantly at Terry as though daring
the DEA enforcer to cuff him. After all, he was regarded as a visionary in
the world of the computer industry. However, his vision proved very
narrow, caused by his drug involvement, that he could no longer see
many far-sighted competitors getting the edge in this volatile high-tech
business. As a result, thousands of his loyal employees were laid off,
many in their 50s and 60s at a time and age when it was most difficult to
find good jobs.

However, this was the CEO who looked out for only himself and his
cronies. He had arranged a "golden parachute" exit package for himself
and his select executive pals assuring them of millions of dollars if they
were suddenly forced to leave the company. In his own case, this con-
sisted of about four times what his company made annually, which represented the salaries of about 20,000 employees who were ousted from
their jobs recently. The CEO's retirement haul would amount to
approximately $150 million.

He figured while being handcuffed, that unless he was imprisoned
for life, he could still collect his bundle of money when released—in
about five to seven years or perhaps earlier depending on who he or
his associates could bribe. He sneered when Terry led him outside in
front of many employees who were probably applauding inwardly.
But, like always, he didn't care what they thought at this point. In
fact, he felt like giving them all the "bird." He figured that by buying a

good lawyer he might even be free to start spending his horde in only a matter of months.

All but chief Cermak were nabbed at the beginning of this purge. He must have heard through his drug network that his police days were numbered and fled the scene. However, Paulson believed he knew where to catch his old boss and was helping the DEA track him down. At last report, the chief was seen in Bogota. Interpol was notified but everyone felt it would be months before Cermak would be brought back to face charges. After all, he knew all the tricks about how to elude capture and avoid extradition.

During this time, Al Benjamin was busy tapping out copyrighted stories locally and to the wire services on his outdated word processor about this dramatic Twin Cities drug scenario. He felt somewhat guilty about the chief getting away. Perhaps he should have been more forceful in his articles about his suspicions regarding Cermak's involvement. Investigators should have been aware that the chief might flee. He was upset that no one was really keeping a good eye on Cermak

Al's nephew, of course, was keeping very close tabs on his uncle. He kept him updated on what was happening and warned him not to break stories that would give any of those involved a chance to escape the law. Indeed, Joe shrugged, Zack Crimmons probably already knew well in advance that the feds were hot on his trail.

In fact, Joe asked for special police protection for his uncle until this scenario became old news. But Al declined the offer, despite Kay's pleas. Almost every day since the scandal hit the press, Joe would check in with Al as though he had some fresh news to report to him—but mostly to make sure his favorite uncle was still okay.

As an investigative reporter, Al was at his best when exposing crime, even if his writing was suddenly interrupted at times by threatening phone calls from unknown sources. Doctor Nancy and Sapel, it seems, had many friends on their side. And some were furious over Al's articles implicating Klein and Sapel with the murders and drug involvement.

As for Loring, his body was never recovered. Police were still trying to determine if it got snagged on the bottom of the deep lake. However, Joe felt the old s.o.b. may have been able to survive and swam to safety.

The worst incident for Al came one night when a bullet crashed through the window of his home office shattering glass all over his work station where he often wrote some of the stories. From then on he made sure his curtains were drawn and that his late night work was kept to a minimum. He felt more secure working among his fellow reporters at the paper now and this also seemed to help his creative juices flow when describing some of the events relating to the drug ring.

But despite all his information, including almost daily inside input from the cops and federal agents, Al couldn't give his readers as much as a hint as to where Zack Crimmons might be holding out. Like the chief, Zack was indeed a slippery ass. He was probably the one who made off with most of the drug money, Al theorized. In fact, his daughters were as puzzled about Zack's whereabouts as were Al and the cops. He left no trace, nor did he confide in any of his pals where he might be headed when the raid began.

All anyone knew for certain was that Zack was missing along with many millions of dollars taken from the International Canadian Bank. But despite such concerns, all Joe could focus on now were wedding bells and happy times.

CHAPTER 26

Zack Crimmon's mind, however, was far from thoughts of weddings. He was too busy planning his next move to escape the law, although getting somewhat weary of being only about one step ahead of the feds. When Benjamin's articles began circulating and were picked up nationally by the wire services, he made it a point to be nowhere around the country. Instead, he quietly found a secluded spot aboard an English cruise ship docked for a few weeks off the rocky coast of Bermuda.

However, he did hear about Sarah's upcoming marriage to the cop and didn't dare reveal his whereabouts to her or anyone else. It was a lonely existence, he admitted, but one essential for survival. As soon as possible, he might contact Robert Beck to see if he could join up with his group. However, the thought lingered in his mind that perhaps Beck would not welcome another fugitive in his organization for fear it would be casting yet another shadow on his already shady image.

And if that was the case, Zack knew he could be done away with as mysteriously as Doc DeSantro.

Besides, Zack could go anywhere he now desired. Frankly, he now had more money than he actually knew what to do with. He took out his wallet but instead of looking at the many bills inside he removed an old snapshot of Sarah and Susan smiling at him when they were mischevious little children. He still loved his daughters deeply, even though Alice at times seemed such a terrible burden for him.

Upset over these thoughts, Zack rose from his deck chair, left his drink, and proceeded to the ship's lounge. Finding a stool at the bar, he sat down, ordered another drink and took another look at his little twin girls.

When the waiter gave him a napkin with his drink Zack reached for his pen, as though intending to idle some time away by "doodling." Instead, however, he immediately began writing on the thin paper like a kid with crayons. His pricey ball point enabled his scratching to be seen clearly.

He became so absorbed in this, he didn't even look up when the waiter returned to see if he was ready for a refill. After a few minutes, he finished writing and then tucked the scribbled napkin in his vest pocket next to his wallet—which contained a Bahamian driver's license, the same license he also had in his possession when he ran into the notorious Pelot one night jogging along a road.

Among the words written on the napkin were: "I hope you like your wedding present Sary." Sary was his pet name for Sarah. "Sus" was his nickname for Susan. He beckoned to the waiter that he was ready for his bill and removed his checkbook to cover the bar charge. The tip he left was excessive, but it was far overshadowed by the next two checks he wrote as soon as the waiter departed.

Zack covered the writing of the other checks with the palm of his hand, making sure no one could observe him as he thoughtfully and slowly filled them out. They also took a much longer time to write than the bar check—for each was made out for $20 million, one for Sarah and the other for Susan. The money was to be withdrawn from the International Canadian Bank,of course, which Zack now did "business" with around the world and which was his prime money-laundering source.

He then arose from his stool and went to his plush cabin, on the main deck of the luxurious HMS cruise liner. Removing an envelope from a desk drawer, he signed "daddy" at the end of the folded napkin and added a note: "Please don't hate me too much." He then jotted his daughters' address on the envelope and sealed it tightly.

With that he quickly packed a bag and headed out the cabin without locking the door or even looking back. The bag was heavy but he didn't have to go far. His first stop was to the ship's drug store where he found a mail drop. He carefully deposited the envelope, which had no return address.

He then headed toward the lounge again but went in another direction which took him next to the outside railing of the ship. While deep in thought about the checks, he noticed a crowd of passengers peering from the railing toward some of the Bermuda reefs. Glancing to where many were focusing their binoculars, Zack noticed a group of what appeared to be patrol boats heading toward the ship, which was anchored only about two miles off the Bermuda coastline.

Fortunately, an officer of the ship was passing by and Crimmons got the chance to ask him what was happening. He was told, in a rather arrogant cockney accent, that the ship had received word to allow some U.S.officials on board for an inspection.

"Inspect what?" asked Crimmons, not wanting to see any drug enforcers on board at this time.

"Well, sir," responded the impatient ship's officer, apparently rather annoyed by the questioning, "usually when this happens, there are several loads of police determined to catch someone aboard who may be involved in drug trafficking. I really must be on my way now.

Zack's face paled. After staring at the departing cruise officer in almost disabelief, he walked—almost ran frantically—to the side of the ship as though attempting to be as far away as possible to the oncoming boarding party. He got as far as the stern where he found an opening near a railing to peer out at the other side of the ship. There everything was serene—almost calm. Moreover, from that position, the drone of the liner's engine could barely be heard.

He gazed down at the peaceful water and thought he could see his reflection. He looked quickly away, however, since what he saw looked frightened and cowardly, as if the reflection was emerging from his very soul. His mind flashed back to his kids and Alice. She was always coming up with sayings for the children to live by, he recalled, like most mothers often do. But one saying he could hear over and over again in Alice's voice was: "He who lives by the sword dies by the sword."

Zack could feel his chest tightening and heard his heart pound as the mere thought of getting caught by the DEA scared the living hell out of him. But there was now nowhere else to run, nowhere to hide. He was very much all alone now—no Alice, no kids, no real home, no real friends.

Although it didn't matter now, he realized the reason he was discovered was probably because he was writing so many checks to maintain his pricey lifestyle. Although they had no address on them, the postal mark on the envelopes enclosing the checks could help lead to where they were mailed.

When the DEA officers finally arrived on board, they met with the ship's captain and were given Zack's cabin number. However, knowing that he may be aware of their arrival, the raiding group broke up and began inspecting every nook and corner where Zack might be found, especially in the bar and lounge sections. Fortunately, one group of these flack-vested searchers encountered the ship officer who only moments before had been talking to the nervous and inquisitive Crimmons.

The officer seemed pleased to describe the man who had been asking about their coming and told them where Zack appeared to be heading. But for the next hour or so, the armed drug enforcers searched throughout the liner with no success. It was only after questioning more of the ship's crew that they had any inkling at all of what may have happened to the elusive person they were so eagerly pursuing.

Both many of the crew and cruise participants informed the searchers that there was a report of a man fitting Zack's description seen near the stern on the main deck who apparently was last observed removing his shoes and socks as thought preparing for a swim. Onlookers tried talking to him, but he yelled at them to get out of his way.

Strangely enough, the shoes and socks were found neatly grouped together near the railing on the deck when the searchers arrived at the scene. Several other people already were there and eager to explain that they had indeed seen a man, who appeared to be in his 50s, climb the railing and jump into the ocean. One woman witness reportedly screamed and the group she was with attempted to throw life jackets to the person floundering in the choppy waters below. However, they reported, he never came up after bobbing in the water several times. It was as if he didn't try to do anything to really save himself, not even holler for help they reported.

The DEA searched both above and under the suface of the water where Zack went down for more than four hours and continued to inspect every nook and cranny of the giant cruise ship for any clues he may have left behind. Although special divers were used, they finally gave up all hope of ever catching him alive and being able to jail him. Like Judge Sims, the slippery Zack Crimmons was logged in as simply a "drowning victim."

About the main difference in the two drownings, besides apparent suicide, was that witnesses claimed to have seen scads of money—all sorts of green currency—floating to the surface in the area where Zack's body hit the water. Some of the bills appeared to be in a variety of denominations, many foreign to their eyes.

They also reported seeing labels on many of the bands around the floating bills. One observer even claimed he spotted the initials "CB", the symbol of the Canadian Bank, on some of the wrapping around the bills. A few of the wrapped bills were fished out by the feds in search of the body, but most sank with the heavy bag Zack was clutching while thrashing about in the water.

Strangely, however, a key was found under the label of one of the money bands recovered from the water. The key, with the CB label, closely resembled the type key that reportedly was missing from around the neck of the drowned Judge Francis Sims, investigators later discovered while probing for more clues.

With the departure of Zack, and most of the money, also went the mystery of who it was that finally got the big payoff from the Sims' mysterious drug affair. It was now quite apparent to investigators that Crimmons indeed had his hands in this all along. However, ironically enough—like pirates of old combatting the Bermuda reef with their stolen loot—no one involved in this highly complex case seemed able to hold on very long to all of their ill-gotten "treasure".

As the ship's captain gazed at the calming ripples still gurgling around the area where the victim and bag submerged, some bills remained on the surface—like a final sad reminder that even millions of dollars is unable to save you from "going under." It was indeed a fitting tribute to see some of the bills rising to slowly form a circle around the turbulent water where Zack went down—almost like a green wreath. Some older witnesses near the ship's railing remarked that this reminded them somewhat of the type wreath attached to the doors of many homes years ago symbolizing that someone was dead inside and was being "waked."

As is customary in the British Navy, the captain of the ship saluted smartly and tipped his decorative cap as a gesture of farewell for the recently departed.

CHAPTER 27

Meanwhile Sarah and Joe had no idea all this trauma was happening. As Zack's body, weighted by his heavy bag, hit the ocean floor and the envelope with his checks was already in the process of being mailed from the Bermuda post office, the happy couple's thoughts were focused only on each other. The wedding bells chimed loudly and as the beautiful bride prepared to proceed down the aisle before a packed crowd of well-wishers in the large and highly decorated St. Paul Cathedral, a stately landmark of the city perched high on a bluff overlooking downtown St. Paul.

Unlike the gray, chilly days that hovered over the Twin Cities area when Judge Sims gasped his last breath, the day Kavinsky and Sarah were wed was surprisingly bright and sunny—in fact, not a cloud in the sky to remind any attending of the grim and gloomy drug affair.

Among attendees at the wedding were numerous newspaper reporters and others from the media who knew Al and Joe, as well as law enforcement personnel along with the many friends and relatives of the bride and groom and, of course, acquaintances of the late Alice Crimmons. Since both Joe and Sarah were born, raised and schooled in the area they had many contacts around the metro and suburban communities. Police cars were among the many vehicles surrounding the old church.

Cameras were flashing, as the bride began her walk down the aisle. Substituting for her father was Al Benjamin who gave the bride away with a smile about as long as the bridal train. He was joyful that Joe finally snagged a wife and that the entire drug episode was over—or was it? A shaky black hand held one of the cameras, a very tiny camera with the inscription of a heart and the name Joe. Was it the same one Joe had in the Bahamas and taken away by Beck's henchmen? Only time could tell. But perhaps this huge syndicated drug chain was indeed hard to disconnect once they zero in on anyone who gets in their way.

Any drug concerns at the moment were gone, however "All's well that ends well, darling," whispered Joe. At this, Sarah lifted her veil and smiled at her handsome groom. She then glanced at her sister who was near the front pew. Susan was escorted by federal marshals who granted her wish to be at the wedding before being returned to the courthouse for further hearings and possible arraignment.

"I'm all yours now cop, you've captured my heart and don't ever be fooled about that," Sarah said softly with her head on his shoulder, "Remember, there's only one of me, Joey. I don't have any doubles, but I'll make doubly sure I'm the only one you'll ever really want to love."

The reception that followed turned into an uproarious combined Irish/Polish/Italian marriage celebration, only slightly louder with more frivolity. Champagne and beer flowed as nearly everyone that knew Joe, Al and the Crimmons toasted the dancing newlyweds. As they twirled about, Joe and his bride couldn't help but notice the many gifts piling up around them, but all they could think about was their approaching honeymoon night in the Radisson Hotel downtown. They then would be off to Bermuda for an intensive love affair. Bermuda sounded very romantical to them both.

While all this was happening, the postman was on his way to the new home of Mr. and Mrs. Joseph Kavinsky with an envelope bearing a colorful Bermuda stamp and the new address. He was driving a mail truck that began making weird noises as he turned a corner leading to their neighborhood. Continuing on his rounds, the rather nervous postman, who wore gloves since the Anthrax terrorist threats, left a can of gasoline in his truck if he ever needed emergency fuel and began noticing smoke coming from under the hood. One glance at his oil gauge showed that it was empty. The sputtering engine was rapidly overheating even in this wintry weather.

He quickly opened the hood and found flames shooting out. But in only seconds the engine was engulfed in fire. What could he do? He was in a residential area where the nearest fire department was miles away. Without a cell phone, he ran to a nearby house to call a suburban fire truck. But by the time the suburb's volunteer fire fighters came, the vehicle and everything in it—including Zack's checks and dreams for eventually making things right for the daughters he so long neglected—had gone up in smoke.

The End

0-595-20981-5